Never give up your dreams.

THE AMULET

A HISTORICAL FICTION NOVEL

by

Dolores Else

Also by Dolores Else

The Women of Burgundy Street

Published by Dolores Else
Cover Design by Nancy Donahue
Interior Formatting by Author E.M.S.
ISBN-13: 978-0-9890256-1-4

Published in the United States of America.

Dedication

To my daughters,

Veronica, Kimberly, and Chrystal

Acknowledgments

I want to thank the gracious people of the city of New Orleans for all of their wonderful hospitality and, as always, their inspiration.

I want to thank the librarians at The Williams Research Center who always go through every precaution to find me the exact information I need, and especially my Reference Librarian, Pamela Arceneaux who leads me in the right direction.

Contents

Camelia

Chapter 1

New Orleans, 1902…

On a tropical, thunderous night in the dim candlelight of Camelia's boudoir, their eyes fastened on the statue of St. Mary on Camelia's small altar in the corner. Unmindful of the storm, her three dearest friends joined her for this service. They always started with a prayer to St. Mary and progressed to their voodoo chants, combining their voodoo beliefs with their Roman Catholic religion. But they hid it from the priests. These services were behind closed doors.

"Hail Mary full of grace! The Lord is with thee;"

And then The Apostles' Creed. "I believe in God, the Father Almighty, Creator of heaven and earth;"

Each of the women placed flowers on the altar and removed their shoes. Camelia offered a small bottle of brandy on the altar and took one of the small drums from the floor, patting it to the rhythm of a dance. She rose and padded through her flat to the beat of her drum while her friends followed through the parlor and into her dining room. They shuffled with more movement of the hips than of the feet, backward and forward, while chanting.

> Atibon Legba Open the gate for me
> Papa Legba Open the gate for me
> Open the gate that I can enter
> God Legba Open the gate for me
> When I return, I will thank the Loa

As thunder roared outside, raindrops plunked on the double windows, and the gasolier flicked dimmer. The women made an offering of candies, fruits, and orris powder on the dining table.

Camelia's tan skin glowed in the luster of the fluttering voodoo candles, as she prepared to make an amulet. A few wisps of gray hair lay on the side of her soft face that had found their way from the white tignon wrapped around her dark hair. She had inherited her small nose and thin lips from her white grandfather. Her two daughters, one from a black man and one from a quadroon, had acquired her same facial features.

Large tourmaline beads showed off their colors in greens and blues at her throat, while ruby glass beads dangled on her chest against her white caftan.

Her friends considered her a wise woman, because she always cured their ills and understood how to soothe their every day worries. They thought she had special powers because she always made them feel better. Camelia didn't believe she knew anything more than any other woman.

She had learned about herbs from her mother and grandmother, and her second husband's mother. Camelia had used her healing skills as a nurse in the War Between the States, making painkillers and salves for the soldiers' wounds. She believed anyone could have done what she had done, if only they worked as hard as she had.

Taking pieces of red satin material that were stitched on three sides, she filled the little pouches with herbs. "See, I just have to stitch one side, and I'll be done."

She knew her friends' problems because she cared about them and asked. Her belief was that anyone could know what their friends were about if they cared enough and used the good sense God had given them.

Camelia turned to her friend Lily. "Please give peace and contentment to our sister, Lily, here. She has been a patient wife to an impatient man most of her life and a doting mother to her daughters and dear son, Elmo." She raised her arms in prayer. "Please, take the grief from her heart from losing a grandchild. Heal her broken heart. I know you will be merciful. Oh, and please fill her home with grandchildren."

"Amen," the women responded.

Lily wore a black mourning dress. Her blue eyes looked up at Camelia, as if she had forgotten something. She sighed with the squeeze of Camelia's reassuring hand. Her tightly curled hair, cut short, and full lips betrayed her pale skin.

"Lily, take this amulet here, and put it underneath your dear son, Elmo's pillow for ten days before their marriage. It will make his seed more potent." Camelia handed Lily the small red, satin pouch. "I will also put an amulet under my daughter, Rosalia's pillow for ten days before their marriage to make her more fertile. And I will see that they select the proper time of the month to get married." She smacked her palms together. "That oughtta do it!"

Lily's mouth widened into a full smile. "Oh, Camelia, you do think of everything, don't you, now?"

Camelia turned to her right to look into the pale face of her dear young friend, Katia. She knew Katia wondered what life held in store for her. "Please give this child the life that a young woman should have to enjoy all the sweet experiences life has to offer. She is an innocent child and does not deserve the disappointments that were handed out to her. Bring her a new life full of happiness."

"Amen," the women responded.

"Katia, my dear friend, I'm going to give you this here amulet and pray you find the life that makes you happy and fulfilled."

"Thank you, Miss Camelia. Your love and friendship has meant so much to me. Ever since I was a little girl, you have guided me, and I love you for that."

"Last but not least, my precious daughter." Camelia looked toward Collette.

As Collette opened her eyes and looked across the table to her mother, her radiance shone. Camelia knew she was looking at a woman in love who had more to offer a man and a child than most. Camelia was proud that this beautiful, quadroon woman was her daughter. She prayed that God would give Collette the child that she so desperately wanted.

"I know what you have been praying for and trying for." Camelia winked in her direction with a nod of her head, and Collette grinned. "You will keep trying to carry Dominique's baby in your body, and if we pray hard enough, it will happen."

Collette's eyes sparkled with excitement at the mention of her beloved Dominique and the baby she wanted to conceive. "That's the best news I've heard in a long time!" She sprung from her chair and ran to her mother, hugging her and kissing her cheek.

They heard slamming in the kitchen, as thunder grumbled outside. Their eyes turned from Collette to La Fonda, a tall, black girl, rushing into the room and finding her place in an empty chair.

"I just now got Blossom Rose to quiet down and go to sleep. I didn't want to leave her with Gossie all havin' a fit or anything. Am I late?" La Fonda peered across the table at Camelia.

"It's fine, La Fonda," Camelia said. "You did right in putting Blossom Rose to sleep first. We prayed and asked for what everyone here wants. You're all so close to me. I know you well and love you all and know God won't disappoint us."

"And I love you too, Miss Camelia. You been better to me than a mother, I'm sure. You know what this wonderful woman has done for me?" La Fonda looked across the table at three eager faces. "She birthed all three of my babies herself. Yes, ma'am." She nodded. "And if it wasn't for her, I probalee wouldn't even have my sweet little baby, Blossom Rose."

"We won't go into that now, La Fonda," Camelia said. "Grab hold of Katia's and Collette's hands and pray."

La Fonda pinched her eyes shut, as she clutched the women's hands.

"Let's pray for dear La Fonda here, orphan and mother of three dear children, raising them as best she can with what you've given her, and she's doin' a damn good job of it if I must say so myself."

"Amen."

"La Fonda, is there something in particular that you'd like to pray for?" Camelia asked.

"Oh, I don't know. I just want for my family to be healthy and happy and for Andre to find a good job. We need a bigger place and all. And I want for my children to go to school and learn to be smart like their father. You know, Miss Camelia."

Camelia nodded. "Please find Andre a job and see to it that La Fonda's children will go to school."

"Amen," the woman prayed.

"Has Andre got that teaching job he applied for yet?" Camelia waited for an answer.

"No, Miss Camelia. He's out workin' for the smithy on the next block. It's just for tonight. He hasn't found anything better. Do you think he will?" Wrinkles formed in La Fonda's brown brow.

"La Fonda, we don't always get exactly what we want, when we want it, but God has a way of giving us what we need. It will work out. Take this little pouch and put it under your pillow and pray."

"How about you, Camelia? What do you want?" Lily looked across the table at Camelia.

"I want for my dear daughter, Rosalia, to find happiness with your son, Elmo. I'd like to see a marriage for them. I'm sure it's in the making. He's courting her tonight. He always shows her such a good time, sweet man. Why, maybe they're setting their wedding date this very minute."

Lightning and thunder crashed at the windows, shaking them in their seats, breaking the silence in the cold room. The gasolier swayed back and forth and spluttered. Its lights went out. Then, a mysterious whiff of air passed over them, leaving Camelia's friends shivering. They blinked in the murky shadows and held tightly to one another's hands.

Camelia's big cat, Bubba, screeched. His gray fur stood on end, his tail straight up. He jumped down from the sideboard and darted between the ladies' ankles under the table, creating a moving sensation.

Katia let out a cry, and the others startled at his slight thumping around their feet. They felt a whoosh of air pass over them as they sighed out loud. The scent of incense wafted in the room, overpowering the freshly baked apple cake and date nut pudding cooling in the kitchen. A gurgling sound echoed in their ears, as their hearts pounded faster.

Camelia gave in to painful thoughts of Claudio, her fourth husband. They had been plaguing her mind. "Oh, I keep seeing him being thrown off that wild horse—that devil! I hope he didn't suffer before he died. Oh, I can't get rid of that scene—him lying on the ground unable to move."

La Fonda's eyes bulged in her small brown face. A chill slid up her spine. "Oh, my. Oh, Miss Camelia, something mighty strange is happening here. Miss Collette, don't let go of my hand."

"Camelia, what's happening? Could we get some light?" Lily asked.

"The lights will go on again. This is just a temporary darkness. Please don't panic, ladies. The gaslights sometimes go out when it rains." A bright zigzag of lightning lit up the room. Thunder cracked like a whip on the windows.

The storm raged like a roaring giant, circling the room. Then, a clicking sound, cleats tapping on a hardwood floor surrounded them, as they looked around the shadowy room in amazement. But Camelia's dining room floor was covered with a soft rug, which made the sounds ghostly. The gasolier lights flashed on and off.

As the lights flickered, Camelia looked toward the windows to see if someone was tapping a coin on the windowpane. She saw a shadowy face of a man in a white suit through the rain, streaming down the windows. At first, her heart skipped a beat, but then she recognized him.

The women looked at one another in fright, as they saw the scare in Camelia's eyes suddenly replaced with serenity through the flickers of the two voodoo candles still lit.

"Oh, my," Camelia declared. "It's you. Isn't it, Claudio? You're okay?" The tap answered. It beat in a rhythmic dance across the windows.

"I feel him caressing my cheek with his beard. I do. Oh, Claudio, it's you. I know it's you. Claudio, I haven't heard from you lately. I was worried I may not hear from you again. You know how I miss you."

The tapping continued, as it entered the room and danced across the walls. Soon, all four walls echoed tap dancing. The guests were mesmerized with the dancing walls and the tapping danced up to the ceiling. Clicking sounds echoed above them, as they looked up, but they could not see the dancer. The gasolier flicked on and off like a neon light. The tapping slithered across the ceiling and then descended down the walls in a steady rhythm. It stopped momentarily and started again more vigorously. Dancing cleats stomped and stomped as if on a hard floor.

The women looked toward the kitchen with the door open a crack. *Was he tap dancing in the next room?* Then, the sounds grew fainter and fainter until they finally disappeared into the soft carpet.

"Oh, he says he loves me. I love you too, Claudio!" Camela's heartbreaking sobs replaced the mysterious tapping.

Another whoosh of air passed above them. All that was left were raindrops, tinkling on the windowpanes. The gasolier suddenly flared brilliantly, and everyone, now visible, appeared relieved.

Camelia looked across the table at her guests. "Well, I guess my prayers were answered much sooner than I had expected."

The restless clopping of a horse's hooves came to a stop outside. "Oh, that must be Rosalia and Elmo coming home. I can't wait for them to come in and announce their wedding date."

When Camelia went into the kitchen to put the coffee on, she found La Fonda at the door close to tears.

"Miss Camelia, I have to leave. If Andre comes home, he'll wonder where I went and ask what was so important to leave my children. I can't lie to him."

Camelia flinched. "Who's asking you to lie?"

"You know he doesn't believe in voodoo or amulets. I don't want to upset him. I have to go before he comes home. I'm sorry."

Drawn to the chanting in the next room, Camelia joined her friends where they prayed for La Fonda.

Rosalia and Elmo sat in silence, as their carriage stopped in front of Camelia's home. Elmo's hand moved to Rosalia's small, rounded breast, cupping it tenderly. Her whispered, "No!" and her push of his hand away from her breast yanked him back to reality.

Oh, she is shy. She has never had a man touch her before. How insensitive of me.

He noted her quivering lip, and her anguished look made him ill at ease. "Oh, I am so sorry, *chere*. Will you forgive me for my ungenteel behavior? I want so to touch you. I thought perhaps you wanted me too, since we're betrothed. Won't you at least look at me?"

She looked away with glassy eyes.

"Don't you ever want me to touch you, to feel your body against mine?" he asked softly.

"I don't want to talk about it."

"We will have to start talking about how we feel about one another soon, since we're to be married in a short time. *Mere* is asking for a wedding date. Don't you ever want to hold me in your arms, to touch the side of my face, or to initiate a kiss?"

She avoided his eyes and kept her silence.

"It is not bad to have feelings for your husband-to-be, *chere.*"

I know that, Elmo, but I simply cannot speak of it. Not now."

"I understand, *ma cherie*. Perhaps another time when you're feeling better."

"Could we bid one another good night now, Elmo, and not go inside together and have everyone confronting us with questions about our wedding date? I'd like to think about it for awhile."

"Of course, *chere*. May I have one small kiss from you to know you forgive me?"

She brushed his lips lightly with hers, as he caressed her cheek.

"I'll send the carriage back for my mother. I'm sure she'll want to talk with you a bit." He looked at her with longing in his dark eyes.

She started to object.

He raised his palm in response. "I'll not interfere I know you have women's issues to discuss."

He helped her out of the carriage and walked her to the front door. "I know," he said. "I won't be going in."

Chapter 2

In their bed, Collette looked up to Dominique with eyes that glistened in the candlelight. "It was a very good meeting. Mamma prayed for a baby for us."

Dominique leaned over her, holding a towel, and dabbed at her wet hair. "You're sure you didn't catch a chill, ma *cherie?* I shouldn't have let you go out on such a terrible night."

"I love the thunder and lightning, *mon cher.* It added excitement to the evening. Mamma even felt my papa in the room when the gasolier went out. We heard him dancing in the dining room. It was splendid.

"Mamma gave all of us amulets. We prayed for a better life for La Fonda and her children and a better future for Katia. Also a marriage ahead for Rosalia and Elmo and children for them. Lily was very happy about that. She wants the patter of little feet running about her home."

As he came to lie next to her, she turned to stroke his naked body and hairy chest. He gingerly removed her nightgown, felt her firm breasts and flitted his fingertips across her nipples, the way she liked it. His hand reached down to smooth her flat stomach and run his hands across her bush and then his fingers moved inside of her. When she started to move her body from one side to the other, he knelt before her between her legs and raised them. He kissed her ankles and calves, as he fondled them. The softness of her light-caramel skin excited him. So alive and warm compared to the pale, cold skin of his first wife, Tess.

"Do you think it will happen for us, *cher?*"

"Yes, my darling, it will. I am thankful it did not happen right away. We have had a wondrous time making love. Trying to make a baby with you has been the joy of my life. I will put life into your body. I promise."

He held her legs up and placed the towel beneath her. He slipped his hardness into her and with each thrust, her body quaked to his hard movements. "Ah, *ma cherie,* my love! My seed will help you blossom!"

"Oh, yes, my sweet. To feel you inside of my body! Oh! It makes me feel loved by you and reminds me how life will feel inside of me. I love you!"

As he made love to her, she moaned in pleasure. The rain pelted the windowpane to the syncopation of her whimpers of passion and Dominique's hard thrusts into her soft, trembling body.

"*Cher*, this is like the first time you made love to me. It was a night like tonight. The rain came down fast. Oh, that was such a memorable night when you first touched my breasts and made love to me."

"But it was different."

"Different?" She looked up to his adoring eyes and wrinkled her forehead in question.

"Yes. It was your first time, and I could not glide into you and out of you, as I do now. Oh, you feel splendid, *ma cherie.*"

As he slid in and out of her, her belly finally rose. Her gasp held her body still. It told him she had reached her peak. He continued making love to her, now a bit faster, as his passion rose, and his breathing quickened. Life stood still for him in the moment that he also peaked and let go inside of her. He smiled down at her glistening eyes. "I remember when you told me it was the first time for you, and I would always be the only one."

"Yes, I remember," she said as she pulled him tighter against her naked body and kissed him openmouthed.

She stroked his backside while listening to the rain pounding harder upon the windowpane.

Dominique wrapped her in his arms, enjoying the taste of her mouth, the smell of lavender on her hair. He prolonged the kiss. "I love you, my darling sweet wife. Life is paradise with you."

"I love you, too, my sweet husband." She slipped the little red satin pouch, which lay beside her, under her pillow. And she wondered if mamma's voodoo would work this time.

Up in their attic flat, La Fonda and Andre were putting Gossie, Geetie, and Blossom to sleep in bedrolls on the floor. "Scoot over, Gossie. Make room for your sisters," La Fonda said.

"Mamma, I've moved as close to the wall as I can. There's no more room."

"Get your arms inside," Andre told Gossie. "And you two angels, Geetie and Blossom, snuggle close together to keep yourselves warm."

"Are you all snug as bugs in a rug? La Fonda asked.

"Yes, Mamma."

"Mamma, are we going to move like I heard Father tell you?" Gossie poked his head out of his bedroll.

"Yes, Gossie, we're going to move and get a fine place to live as soon as I get a better job," Andre said. "Then, you won't have to sleep on the floor. You will all have your own beds."

"Father, when we move, will I be able to go to school? I'm almost eight now."

"Yes, Gossie. We'll get you into school soon," Andre promised his son. "Come to bed, Mamma."

La Fonda dropped the red satin pouch into the trunk, burying it under their clothes before blowing out the candle so that Andre wouldn't see it.

"What are you doing there?" Andre asked as he got into bed.

"Nothing." La Fonda slipped into bed.

Andre drew La Fonda close to his body. The warmth of her body and the smell of laundry soap on her skin excited him. "Come closer, *cherie*," he whispered.

He pulled up her nightgown, and she held him tight, feeling his warm body next to hers. Their lips met in hungry passion. He slipped into her and moved in and out of her ardent body. She welcomed his body into hers, as she pressed him closer to her with her arms around his back. They slid in and out as quietly as they could in their passion. His arousal stirred his emotions, as he called out to her, *"Cherie, je t'adore."*

Gossie opened his eyes to his father's love words. "Father."

"Yes, Gossie."

"I don't mind sleeping on the floor. Honest. I'm just so happy that you're living with us now. That's the best thing that could ever happen. And I don't care if we never move from here, as long as you live with us."

Katia stepped down from the carriage onto Eva's courtyard. She approached the door by the light of the coachman's lamp. The door opened to Eva's greeting.

"Katia, you're out in the worst storm of the year. Why ever did you go out on a night like tonight?"

"Oh, Eva, let me tell you all about it."

Katia entered through the women's entrance, which led to Eva's boudoir. She felt the warmth of the fire in the fireplace, as she shivered. "It's so nice in here compared to the coach. I'm cold."

"Tati is making a fire in your room. Let's go upstairs, where you can take your wet wraps off." Leading Katia into the hall, and up the staircase with a kerosene lamp, Eva walked down a hallway and opened a door to a guest room to find a black servant stoking a fire in the fireplace.

"Come in, please, Miss Katia and Mommy Eva. It should be toasty for you now, Miss Katia." The flames of the fire gilded Tati's copper face and presented an infectious smile, as she turned to face them.

"Oh, Tati, you're a godsend." Katia removed her cape and started for the armoire.

"Let me take that for you, Miss Katia. I've laid out your nightgown and chenille robe on the bed." Tati took Katia's wet cape and hung it in the armoire away from the other clothes.

"Oh, you think of everything, Tati. Thank you." Katia turned to Tati with gratitude and hugged her.

"I will leave you now. Is there anything I can bring you?" Tati looked at the two women eager to wait on them.

"No, you've done more than I could want," Katia said. "Thank you again."

As she undressed behind a folding dressing screen and put on her nightgown and robe, Katia gushed with excitement. "Eva, you should have been there. It's too bad you had a previous engagement. Camelia gave me an amulet to put under a chair cushion when I meet the man I want to marry. What do you think of that?"

"I think it's quite possible, *chere*. I say it's your time to meet someone wonderful."

"And she gave me this amulet for you to put on your altar. Perhaps in time, you will also learn to trust a man."

"I think my time has passed. But then yours is yet to come," Eva said in self-denial.

"I don't know why you say that, Eva. You are still young and very beautiful. Oh, I wish you had been there tonight to witness the eeriness.

"Camelia's fourth husband, Claudio, was communicating with her. He was dancing on the windows, which cracked as the thunder roared outside. It was glorious. And right there on the ceiling in the very room we were sitting in, dancing went on. Can you imagine? We could hear it as plain as you can hear me talking."

Katia walked to her bed and lay on her stomach. She patted the bed and looked up to Eva, sitting in a cushiony chair.

Eva joined Katia, sitting next to her. "I think Camelia is good for you. I don't ever remember seeing you this happy, Katia."

"Eva, Camelia would ask him a question and dancing would start in the rhythm of one of the songs they used to dance to. Camelia would recognize the rhythm. And she felt him caressing her cheek. And we could all feel the whoosh of air pass over us." Katia flitted her fingers like butterflies flying over her head. "The gasolier flickered on and off when he was dancing. Oh, I do wish you could have been there to hear it."

"It sounds intriguing. I'm happy for you, Katia. Things are starting to happen for you now with your new dress shop business."

"Yes, I'm excited! I must get to my shop early in the morning. I have fabrics coming in, and Camelia has agreed to do the alterations."

"You haven't forgotten that you've agreed to close the shop some time to go for a holiday with me to my plantation house, have you? I want to introduce you to my cousin, Justice."

Katia's brow furrowed. "I've got so much to do to get my dress shop started. Camelia has recommended my shop to her neighbors. Some of them have indicated they want to buy dresses. If they purchase dresses, I'll have to fill the orders before I leave. When was it you were planning to go?

"The week after next."

Katia bit her lip and shrugged. "I'll do my best to get dresses fitted, altered, and delivered by then. Really, I will, Eva."

Chapter 3

The turn of events kept going round in her mind as Rosalia fed the birds, who didn't seem as hungry as usual this morning. She watched as the sparrows pecked at the bread cubes, wondering why everyone expected her to make a change in her life. Her mother and Lily couldn't wait for her to marry Elmo and have a child so that they could have a grandchild. *Why must I replace the grandchild that Lily lost? Does Elmo really want this? Will he do anything to please his mother?*

Elmo is a good man. I like being courted by him, but do I want to get married?

"Oh, there you are," Camelia called out from the side stairway of the building. "I wondered where you had gone." She rushed to the courtyard. "Rosalia, *chere*, you haven't had your breakfast yet. Do come in from the damp breeze and have some hot coffee with me."

"In a minute, Mamma." Rosalia glanced sadly at the sparrows before following her mother to the front flat where they lived. When she entered the kitchen by the back door, she saw that her mother had poured coffee in two large cups accompanied by a plate of fresh *biegnets* and a tray of sliced apples and cheese. She had no appetite, but she would have coffee with her mother.

"Sit," her mother encouraged. "I want to hear all about last night's activities. Did he take you to a dance?"

"Yes, he did, Mamma."

"Did he take you to supper?"

"Mamma, they had food at the dance, more than we could possibly want. After eating at the dance, we wouldn't have been able to eat another bite."

"Oh, I know. Elmo would have taken you some place nice to eat if you hadn't already eaten. Rosalia, have a *biegnet*. Please."

Rosalia took a *biegnet* from the plate to please her mother.

"Now, tell me, *chere*. Did he ask you again about setting a date for the wedding? We're all anxious to know."

"Yes, he did."

"And?" Camelia looked across the kitchen table at her daughter's downcast eyes.

"I said I'd think about it."

"Rosalia," Camelia whined. "What more is there to think about? You're not going to find a better man than Elmo, now, are you?"

"No, it's not that. The question is can Elmo find a better wife?"

"What in the world are you talking about? He's only had eyes for you since Collette's wedding. You know that."

They heard a rap at the kitchen door. Camelia rose to answer it.

"Silas Loutierre at your service, Madame Arceneaux. Come to fix your window pane." The young black man showed a full mouth of white teeth and tipped his hat.

"Why, Silas, how prompt you are. I just told the baker this morning about my broken window. I can't imagine how it got that crack in it. Do come in."

Silas entered the kitchen, hat in hand, and bowed to Rosalia, sitting at the table. "Mornin' to ya, ma'am." He followed Camelia into the dining room to scrutinize the broken windowpane. "Happens. Yeah, sometimes, it jest happens. I can fix it, Madame, twenny cents it'd be ta fix it."

"That'll be fine, Silas."

Rosalia appeared in her cape and announced, "I have to leave, Mamma."

"Where're you going at this time of day?"

"I have an errand. I'll tell you about it later, Mamma."

She rushed past Camelia and left before her mother could ask any more questions.

Silas still stared at the windowpane, scowling, wondering how the window cracked since it was too high for a person to break from the outside. He pulled out a piece of glass from a felt sack and held it up against the window. "Yep, it'll fit. I could do this. Yes, an' anythin' else ya need fixin'. I clean chimneys, too. Ya need yer chimneys cleaned, Madame?"

Camelia, sitting in a dining chair, started to do her hand sewing. "I don't believe I'll have them cleaned

today, Silas. Maybe next time. I sure am happy you're
fixing that window. Why not even an hour ago, I told
the baker I needed a fixit man. You must not come
from very far."

"No, ma'am. I jest live up three, fow blocks up
thataway."

"On Burgundy?"

"Yes, siree."

"Who's your mamma?" Camelia leaned forward,
peering over her reading spectacles.

"My mamma's Melba Loutierre." His gloved hand
gingerly removed the jagged shards.

"Well, wouldn't you know it? You're Melba's boy!
Your mamma used to be a dear friend of mine. Why,
I sewed your mamma's wedding dress and her
bridesmaid's dresses, too. We used to go out together,
your mamma and daddy and my Rufus and me. How
are your mamma and daddy? It's been so many
years."

"My daddy died 'bout twenny years ago. I was jus'
a little boy, yes ma'am."

"Oh, I'm so sorry. Has your mamma remarried?"

"No, my mamma's been alone all this time."

"That's too bad. And you, Silas, have you ever
married?"

"I was married to the sweetest, prettiest woman
in the whole world and she died havin' our little
angel from heaven. Lost my little angel too—a little
boy."

"Oh, I'm sorry to hear that. It must be lonely for
you."

"Yeah. I'm like a fish outta water since my wife died. My mamma asked me to come back home, so I'm back with her now."

"Is your mamma well?"

"No, she's havin' her problems. Gettin' up in age now, you know."

"I'd love to see her. We were such dear friends at one time. Silas, could you do me a favor and ask your mamma to come see me?"

"I could do that for you, madame, but my mamma don't get out much any more. Got the lumbago, you know. Can't hardly walk from her bed to the kitchen. Some days she stays in bed because she can't stand the pain." He shook his head. "Pitiful, just pitiful."

An idea struck Camelia, as she laid her hand sewing down. "Oh, I can give her something for that. I'll get my herbs ready to take to her and put them in my bag so I won't forget them." She ran to her kitchen. "I've got to go see your mamma, as soon as I finish that dress. I can't wait another day. What a thrill it'll be to see her again after all these years."

The polished headstones shimmered from the early morning rain as Rosalia walked between them and looked for her father's. She stepped carefully, avoiding puddles, as she read the headstones.

She spotted her father's name, Rufus Bailleaux, born 1835, died 1901. With a hammering heart, she fell to her knees and gritted her teeth. A gnawing feeling came over her, as she held in a sob and then let loose a piercing shriek. She grabbed a fistful of wet grass and dirt and threw them at her father's headstone. "Why? Why? Why didn't you stay away? What monstrous spell did you have on my mother? Why? Why?"

Her body quivered at the graveside, as she wailed in mournful agony. "Rapist!" she screamed. "That's what you were! I hate you for what you did to me!"

Rosalia

Chapter 4

When Camelia knocked on her front door, she heard Melba's voice yell out over the fruit peddlers, hawking in the street.

"Camelia? Come on in."

As she entered the parlor, Camelia barely recognized the gray-haired black woman, sitting in a rocking chair, her shoulders crouched, clutching a shawl. Still, her voice sounded familiar.

"My boy told me you'd be comin' today. I can't believe it's you after all this time.

"Yes. It's me, Melba."

"Sit down." The old woman gestured to the settee next to her.

Camelia slid into the horsehair-filled upholstered chair and reached out to a cold hand. "I've wanted to see you for a long, long time and then it was like God sent Silas to my home to fix my window. Strange. We don't know how it cracked, that window."

"Oh, Camelia. You can't imagine how many times I've walked past your house wanting to see you."

Camelia grasped the cold hand tighter, trying to warm it.

"But…" Melba hesitated, groping for the right words to explain what had happened twenty-nine years ago when she had gone off with Camelia's new husband, Rufus.

"You see, Camelia, I was at a bad time in my life when you and I parted. My Harry wasn't like your Rufus. He didn't know how to treat a woman and make her feel special and proud to walk with him, like Rufus." She winked at Camelia and nodded. "Harry may have cared for me somehow, but he didn't know how to show it. We never had any fun like you and Rufus. So, when Rufus gave me some attention and wanted to kiss me…" She glanced down and shuddered, as she thought of that time long ago and regretted it.

"Well, my Harry never kissed me. When Rufus kissed me, it was like a fly to flypaper. I couldn't let go of him. And one thing led to another, and we ran off to finish what we started. It was at that fair the four of us went to, you, Rufus, Harry and me."

Camelia looked away, her mind off in another time. A happier time. She was twenty-one years of age and newly married. She had lost her first husband, Chester, not quite nineteen years of age, in The War Between the States. Her second husband, Moses, died of the fever. With her third husband, Rufus, she hadn't been a mother yet, but hopeful to conceive. She loved her husband in spite of his roving eye. Yes, she even knew when she was newly married that

Rufus was attracted to other women, and other women were attracted to him.

The ladies loved all the attention he paid them. He was so alive and so much fun to be with, she'd felt at the time. She'd loved how Rufus held her tight when he danced with her. No man had ever danced with her quite like that. The way he'd looked at her that first day she met him had made her heart flutter.

"We only went out about three or four times, Rufus and me, but those times were the most fun I ever had in my life," Melba said.

Melba's confession took Camelia back to the day she'd met Rufus. She thought of his lopsided grin that had attracted her to him, as he ate in a crawfish-eating contest, winning first place. How carefree she'd felt when he took her dancing that night and how he had made her forget her work. He could hold back time. Rufus meant play time.

"Yes, no doubt, he lived for fun and play." Camelia said. "You don't need to remind me of that. Even now, I can see him dancin' his fool head off, challenging anyone crazy enough to try to outdance him, tipping his hat to the ladies, not missing a beat I see him all the time."

"I know. I see him all the time, too." Melba grimaced in a sigh of discomfort.

"You look down in the mouth," Camelia said. "Where's your pain?"

"Where isn't it?"

"That bad?"

Melba rubbed a hand across her backside and up her spine to the nape of her neck.

"Let me help you to your boudoir. You can rest under your duvet, while I go in the kitchen to boil some water for a poultice."

As Melba rested in her room, Camelia returned with two hot poultices and applied one to her sore back, another to the nape of her neck. "Now, just relax, *chere*. The pain will leave you. We'll do this twice a day for the next two or three days and then whenever you need it."

Camelia looked down into Melba's withered face, seeing years of pain and loneliness. "Do you think you can sit up a little, *chere*, and drink this herbal tea? Here, I'll plump your pillow. You rest your back against it. And I'll place this amulet I made for you in your bed. Keep it there, and pray for health."

As she punched the pillows, Camelia suddenly imagined Rosalia with Silas. "You know, Melba, my Rosalia is getting up there in years. I want to see her married. I just had a thought. Your Silas and my Rosalia could make a mighty pair, couldn't they? She doesn't seem to want to marry the man who's courting her, although I can't imagine why."

Melba's frown agitated Camelia.

"Nay! Melba moaned. "God forbid."

"And why not?" Camelia demanded.

"Read the cards."

"What aren't you telling me, Melba?"

"Can't you see it in his strut, his shoulders pushed back like him, the twinkle in his eyes when he's happy?"

"I've only seen your boy for a few minutes." She stopped cold. "Oh, *Mon Dieu!* You mean he's..."

"Yes, Camelia. He's Rufus's. I couldn't bear to ever tell you. It's still a stab in my heart to admit it. Maybe it's because Harry and I never could have a child. Oh, I shouldna make excuses for my sin. Not to you. I sinned. I'm sorry." She looked up to Camelia with pleading eyes. "But I'm not sorry I had Silas. I really wanted a baby, real bad, but I felt terrible about you. I lost the best friend I ever had in my whole life. I missed you, Camelia."

"I missed you too, Melba."

A proud smile suddenly lightened Melba's somber face. "He's a good boy, isn't he, Camelia?"

"Yes, he is. From what I've seen so far, he's a good man. He's not a boy any more, Melba. He's a man." Camelia paused for a moment, stunned. "Oh, you mean Silas and Rosalia are brother and sister?"

Melba strained to pick her head up and nod. She reached for Camelia's hand and kissed it. "Will you ever forgive me, Camelia?"

"I'm here. Ain't I? I licked my wounds over Rufus a long time ago. Oh, Melba, don't look at me like that. I've forgiven you years ago. He's gone, and we're both still here. I don't understand why in the world we didn't get together sooner. He sure wasn't worth losing you. Now, drink some more of this tea. Just one question, Melba. Did Silas know Rufus?"

"No. I didn't tell him about Rufus for a long time. He thought Harry was his daddy, but when Harry was long gone and Silas was full grown, I told him Rufus was his real daddy. He wanted to see what he looked like. So, I took him down to the square.

Rufus was dancin' his fool head off, like he always did, showing off like a shameless hot dog. I introduced Silas to Rufus as "your boy." Rufus talked to Silas a spell and plunked him a fifty-cent piece and went on his way, struttin' proud as a peacock. He never came around to see the boy. But Silas always refers to Harry as his daddy."

"Yeah. Visiting his children was not one of Rufus's strong points. I always wondered how many of Rufus's offspring ran around town bumping elbows with him."

Melba didn't laugh. She bobbed her head to the beat of her throbbing pain. Lines of misery crisscrossed her forehead as she squinted through the sting of unhappiness.

"Camelia, it was Silas what brung us together."

"Yes, Melba, it was your dear son."

"Bring my cards. They're on the mantle. Set them on this tray here," Melba said.

"Are you going to read my cards, *chere?* Just like you used to?" Camelia hurried from the mantle and set the cards on a bed tray in front of Melba.

"Now, what's been going on in your life? What are you praying about?"

"I told you. I want my Rosalia married, and I pray for her happiness every day. I just don't know what's going on with that child. She has a good man, and she puts him off. Why is she avoiding marriage?"

Melba shuffled the cards in the three-card spread and laid them on the tray. Her eyes widened. "She has had some tragedy in her life. Do you know about that?" Melba looked up at Camelia with inquisitive eyes.

"*Mon Dieu.* Yes. You can see that in the cards?"

"Yes. She has not gotten over this horrible incident in her life. You cannot help her to get over it." Melba pointed to The Hanged Man Card. "See here?"

Camelia looked away with misting eyes. "Yes, I know about that. I still can't talk about it—not even with you."

"That's okay, Camelia. We don't need to go into that right now. This means you must not stand in her way, you or anyone. She must find the way herself. Only then, will she find happiness. I see that your daughter must take a journey. It will not be an easy journey. There will be hardship and tears."

"Why? Why must she do that?"

"She has to learn which path to take. It will be a long road." She pointed to The Hermit Card. "Her journey will lead the way for her to know which path to follow. Leave her to her solitude while she searches for the truth."

"Oh, I hope she will find happiness. My sweet daughter deserves it," Camelia said.

"I see a young friend of hers who eventually leads her in the right direction, only by example, mind you. There will be a girl who will be instrumental in her life, a confidante. This confidante will make her realize what she herself must do. That's all I can tell you." Melba gathered the cards in one pile and shuffled them with dexterity that belied her invalid state. "Do you want me to read *your* cards?"

"No, not for me, but I've been praying for my *blanchiseusse,* the little black girl, the one who lives up in the attic. Well, she's not that little really. She married my nephew, Andre, and they're having a hard time of it."

"Andre? The one who was a priest?"

"Yes, that's the one."

"God forbid." Melba spread her tarot cards out.

"What do you see for her?" Camelia watched Melba's face with curiosity.

"I see the Strength card. This poor girl has had very good inner strength to overcome the worst obstacles. Poverty. Hard work. She has the ability to endure hardship. She has strong faith in God. That's how she has been able to survive."

"What do you see in her future?"

"Oh, *Mon Dieu!* I see illness—terrible illness. Someone will be very sick. Two of Wands. Disease."

"Is it a child?" Terror broke through her voice, and Camelia's eyes widened.

"No, I don't see a child. I see someone lying in bed, but not a child." Melba pondered the card, tapping it with one crooked, sensitive fingertip.

"Oh, Mercy. No. Not more misery in that poor orphan's life." Camelia paced the room and wrung her hands.

"I don't see death." Melba leaned over the edge of the bed and spat on the floor. She spat again. "Don't fret so, Camelia. There will not be a death. I spat it out like I spit out a bitter seed."

"I certainly hope not. I've lost four husbands, and that's enough death to last me a lifetime."

"You will be instrumental in helping them. They will lean on you in more ways than one. See here? You will be the strong one, Camelia."

"Yes, I see."

Sadness covered Melba's face. "Oh, if I could have known to spit out the bitter seed of death for my husband, Harry. Then, my boy could have grown up knowing the love of a father. You know, he loved the boy. And he never knew."

"I'm glad Silas knew the love of a father for longer than my girls. Rosalia and Collette didn't have that much. Rufus left us when Rosalia made four years, and Claudio died in a horse accident when Collette only made two years." Camelia looked up to see Melba's tired eyes drooping. "Let's put the cards away for now." Camelia gathered the cards and put them back on the mantle. "You rest and your back will feel better. I'm going to leave you for now with your tea. I'll be back later."

As Camelia left the room, Melba called out to her, "He wasn't worth it. All these years without you. That Casanova!"

Chapter 5

"Come in, Mamma. Rosalia and Elmo, it's so nice to have you in my home." Collette beamed with happiness, welcoming her family.

"Mamma, Rosalia, come into the kitchen. I have something to show you."

"Let's see what the women are ogling." Dominique waved to Elmo, as he followed.

An oak wall phone hung on a green wall.

"This is a telephone. That's what they call it. Mamma, you could call me from the *pharmacie*. They also have one of these. We could talk to one another every day if you want. See here." She pointed to the crank on the side. "You turn this crank and tell the operator the number you are calling. This is my number here. Write it down." She handed her mother the black earpiece at the end of a wire. "You listen with this, Mamma, and you speak into this."

"My Land! What will they think of next? Dominique, do you have a pencil?" Camelia asked.

"Yes, *mere.*"

"Oh, I just remembered, *chere*. Madame Le Doux in the flat behind me just got a telephone. I'm sure she'll let me use it to call you. Won't that be lovely? I can just walk across the hall from my back door and talk to my little girl when I have a yen to hear your voice."

"It's lovely, Collette. May I try it?" Rosalia asked.

"Here, Sister. Hold it to your ear. If you hear someone talking, then hang this up here. We share the telephone line with another family. So, it's polite to hang up, but if you hear this little buzzing tone, then you can tell the operator the number you're calling."

"I'm so happy I'll be able to call you up," Rosalia said.

Collette looked across the kitchen at Dominique, handing Camelia a pencil. Her eyes glazed over with love for him. He glanced over at her returning his love.

Rosalia turned to Elmo, who reached for her hand, leading her out of the kitchen into the dining room.

As the rest of the family followed, Camelia marveled at how lovely their flat looked. "Your table looks exquisite, Collette."

"Thank you, Mamma. I learned from you. Let's all sit for dinner, please. Elmo, you may sit there, and Rosalia, you may sit next to your fiance."

"I'll help you bring the food in, *chere*," Camelia said.

"Mamma, now you just sit and enjoy. I'll bring dinner in. It's all warm in the oven."

As Collette brought dishes in one by one, Camelia raved about the chicken and sweet potatoes. "This is just the way I like it. So very tasty. And the biscuits are to die for. Wherever did you learn to make them so flaky?"

"Of course, Mamma. It's exactly the way you fix them. The eggplant is your recipe, too."

Laughter poured from the dinner guests. Dominique rose and lifted his wineglass. "I want to toast to my beautiful wife who has given me the happiest year and a half of my life. And to my mother-in-law, the backbone of this family, who raised two charming, god-fearing daughters. And to my sister-in-law, Rosalia, who is like a sister to me. And to Elmo, I welcome you to this wonderful family. I hope we will become brothers."

Rosalia tinkled her wineglass with her dessertspoon. "I have an announcement to make."

Camelia beamed with pride, and Elmo's eyes twinkled with joy.

"I want you all to know I've prayed about this and put a lot of thought into this decision, and…" She looked toward Elmo's glistening eyes and hesitated.

Collette sensed her sister's nervousness, seeing her hesitation. She could almost hear Rosalia's heart pounding in her chest. Rosalia swallowed hard and took a deep breath. She looked across the table at her mother's happy face and Elmo's eyes wide with anticipation. He seemed to try to hide his smile, but it was evident, as he looked at his future bride, how happy he was.

"I've decided to enter the convent." Rosalia nodded as if to reaffirm her words.

As Elmo lifted his chin and looked across the table at her, the words hit hard. His brown eyes held her firmly as if to say *why are you doing this to me? Don't you love me?*

Collette felt the pain slicing through Elmo's heart, but she knew her sister wouldn't back out, now that she had told the family.

Camelia's face stiffened. "But this is so sudden. I thought you wanted marriage."

"Mamma, I thought you would be happy for me. I found my vocation! You were happy for Andre when he found his vocation."

"But that was different. He wasn't planning a marriage. You never spoke of such a calling to me, Rosalia." Camelia's voice rang louder. "Never once."

"I've been thinking of a religious vocation for a time now. I didn't want you to talk me out of it. That's why I haven't spoken of it."

"But what about Elmo and your wedding plans? Lily's been waiting for you to set the wedding date so she can make plans for the reception in her home." Camelia's face grew even more serious.

"I think God should come first in our plans. If we can serve the Lord, that should be at the top of the list." She turned to face him fully for the first time. "And Elmo, dear sweet Elmo, you deserve much better than me."

Shocked, Elmo stared at Rosalia with unspeakable disappointment. He lowered his eyes in humiliation.

"Oh, Rosalia, how could you say such a thing? You are in his eyes every moment you are near him. It is apparent to everyone that Elmo loves you and you love him," Collette said.

"I don't feel I would be the kind of wife Elmo needs." Rosalia looked down at her wineglass, nodding in defiance.

Elmo shot a glance at Rosalia. "You've decided what I would need? I've always felt you were exactly what I needed. Your kind heart. Your humility. Your modesty. Your beauty, but I can see…"

Rosalia's heart sank at the word *beauty. No one has ever called me beautiful but him. Mon Dieu, does he believe I am truly beautiful?*

He rose, bracing his hands on the table. "Please excuse me. I feel this matter is for the family to discuss, and I am an intrusion."

"Oh, are you sure you must leave?" Collette asked. "We haven't even had coffee."

Dominique started towards Elmo. "Please, please, Elmo. You haven't finished dinner. Stay for coffee and brandy. We so enjoy your company. You are never an intrusion. You are part of our family."

Elmo raised his palm. "Please. He swallowed hard. Excuse me." He turned to Rosalia. "I trust you will get home safely with your mother, *ma chere.*" He kissed her on the cheek and wheeled to the door a shaken man, as the family watched dumbstruck.

Chapter 6

Camelia sat in the early morning stillness, staring at the blue-tinged flames leaping in her brick fireplace. Why her daughter had chosen to leave a comfortable life with Elmo to take a vow of chastity, poverty, and obedience was beyond Camelia's comprehension. Rosalia had never spoken to her of a religious life, so why would she choose it now? She heard an insistent knock on her front shutters.

As she opened the front door and pushed the shutters open, she found Lily standing with a plate of cookies.

"My land, Lily. What are you doing here so early in the day? I don't have an alteration appointment with you, do I?"

"Of course not. I just thought you might like some company. I know how hard this is for you, *chere.*" Lily looked into Camelia's swollen eyes.

"Yes, this is the day I've been dreading. I wish I could set free the grief I feel over losing my daughter. Is it selfish of me to want her for myself? I don't know how I could stand to be away from her. We've never been apart, even for a day."

"I know, *chere*. You are the last person in the world I would call selfish. You've been so close to your daughters. I understand how hard this is for you." Lily patted Camelia's hand. "Is she getting ready?"

"Yes, she's in her room." Camelia nodded towards Rosalia's boudoir. "Would you like some coffee?" Camelia gestured to Lily's plate of cookies she had placed on the coffee table.

Lily waved aside the offer.

"May I ask how your son, Elmo, is doing?"

"He doesn't spend much time in the house. Mostly, he mopes in the *garconniere*. He says he wants to be alone. Oh, Camelia, he is devastated. What else can I tell you?"

"I am so sorry." Camelia couldn't help remembering the first time she'd met Lily. "You are my oldest friend, Lily. When I came back to New Orleans after Claudio died in Baton Rouge, you showed me this here flat and rented it to me. You were so gracious, showing me every little thing, like how this fireplace works. And you were so sweet to my little girls. You became my landlady and my best friend, when I needed one the most. You were a godsend, Lily."

"Mamma. Lily." Rosalia nodded to both, as she entered the parlor. "I think I'm ready to go."

"My man is waiting outside in the carriage. I thought it easier to have him drive us," Lily said.

"Oh, you don't have to…"

"Camelia, let me be with you. I don't want you to be alone on your way back from the convent."

They left the house and entered the carriage with the able assistance of Lily's personal driver. Silence permeated the coach. The women did not speak. Camelia felt as if her heart were broken. Lily felt sorrow for Camelia's pain. And Rosalia did not know what to expect in her life, but prayed she would find the answer.

Upon reaching the convent, Camelia led the way, pushing the iron gates open. A knock on the front door soon summoned a young postulant. "Yes, madame?"

The girl in a long black dress with closely cropped hair seemed too young to be wearing a widow's dress in Camelia's eyes. She felt disheartened at the sight of her.

Camelia blinked back tears, seeing Rosalia's dear face instead of the postulant. *She will never know the love of a man, what it feels like to be made love to. The feel of life inside of her. What it feels like to hold a tiny infant to her breast. She doesn't even know what she wants in life.*

The girl repeated, "Yes, madame?"

"Madame Arceneaux calling to bring Mademoiselle Rosalia Baillieux, my daughter, to enter the convent."

"Please, come in."

As the three women entered the convent, an old nun entered the vestibule. "And you are?" She stared into Rosalia's eyes with her arms akimbo.

"I am Rosalia Baillieux."

"Sister. Say Sister, I am Rosalia Baillieux." The nun's scratchy voice and assertive body language was not welcoming.

"Sister, I am Rosalia Baillieux," Rosalia repeated.

"Rita, take Rosalia Baillieux to the dormitory," the nun said.

Rosalia turned to take a last glance at her mother. She kissed her fingers and waved good-bye, looking as though she wished she were anywhere else.

Camelia saw the look of uncertainty and fear in her daughter's eyes. She reached out to her, hoping to change her mind at the last minute.

Rosalia embraced her mother, then Lily. *"Au revoir*, Mamma. *Au revoir*, Lily."

The old nun blocked Camelia's view of her departing daughter. "Come into my office, madames."

Lily and Camelia followed the nun into her office where she gestured for them to sit in front of her desk. "I want to acquaint you with our rules, madames."

"I am Madame Arceneaux, Rosalia's mother, and this is Madame Bennot, a very dear friend of the family."

"Yes. Ahem. Our first rule is that our postulants do not have visitors for the first three months. This will enable them to become acclimatized to their new environment without intrusion from family and friends."

Camelia, barely able to restrain herself, stared at the nun in disbelief. Lily rubbed the top of her friend's hand to soothe her.

The nun continued by rote, staring at the crucifix on the wall, her hands folded as if in prayer. "After three months, visiting hours are once a month the first Sunday from one to three p.m. There are no letters between the postulants and their families and, of course, no telephone calls."

"But what if there is a family emergency like a death in the family?" Camelia asked with fear in her eyes.

"Madame, the postulants must learn that they must separate themselves from earthly things, and that includes their families. They prepare to be brides of Christ and not be concerned with things of this world. Their father is in heaven, not here on this earth," the nun recited in her church-like manner.

Camelia looked eye to eye with the nun. "What if my daughter were to become ill? Certainly, you would let me know, wouldn't you, Sister?"

"We take care of the postulants and the nuns. You won't have that worry any more." The nun's voice was as impenetrable as a glacier.

"But I want to know if my daughter is not well."

"Not to worry, I told you. We take care of them."

"Sister, you see, my daughter, Rosalia, and I have never been separated. I need to know that she is well, or I don't know if I can live, not knowing."

"Madame, this is why we have this three month period of no outside visitors. The girls must adjust when they enter the convent. Three months is not such a long time for you not to see your daughter compared to her lifetime in the convent."

Camelia wrung her hands and restrained a cry of horror.

The nun appeared emotionally blind to Camelia and made her plea for charity. "I understand that you sew for a living. In the case of the veils, our postulants are in dire need of them. Can you take an order from our convent?"

"And may I ask who would pay for the material for the postulant's veils?"

"I'm sure with the wonderful creole clientele that you have, there is someone who would be able to pick up the cost."

"You mean that you want me to solicit my clientele for your purposes, Sister?"

"Madame, surely you can't refuse. It's for the church."

Camelia pulled herself taller. Her brow showed irritation at the nun's ungracious manner. "Who am I talking to, may I ask? Do you have a name?"

"Sister Reginald," the nun replied.

"Sister Reginald, every day of my life, I live and work for three children of a catholic priest. I am not complaining. I do it for love, but I cannot for you. I am not able to pick up the cost. My clientele are Creoles of the highest caliber who keep their word and pay their bills in a timely manner, making my profession that I depend on, a joy to work in. I do not feel that I can solicit my patrons for money. That is not how I do business."

"Then, we are through here, Madames. *Au revoir.*"

Camelia looked at Lily, speechless, before rising and leaving the room with a heavy heart.

Chapter 7

"Silas! Silas! I can't stand it any more. Come down."

"What'd I do now, Miss Camelia?" he called down her chimney from the flat above.

"Just come down. I need to talk to you."

Silas bounded into the parlor, filthy black with soot in his tuxedo attire and stovepipe hat worn over a black woolly cap. "What's you fussin' for?"

"Silas, I am just so miserable, I can hardly stand myself. I miss my baby girl so much, I'm about to die. Could you get a letter to her somehow?"

"Why, I don't rightly know, Miss Camelia. Where she at?"

"She's at the Holy Family Convent preparing for her vows, and the Mother Superior won't let me visit her, and she can't get mail." Camelia paced her parlor back and forth, holding her forehead. "Don't you clean chimneys there or know one of the chimney sweeps on Orleans Street?"

Silas squeezed his sooty eyelids shut, trying to think of the quadroon convent area on Orleans Street. He knew all of the chimney sweeps in town and tried to think of who worked there.

"Well, Silas. Do you? This is very important. I can't go another day without communicating with my daughter. I've never been away from her more than a few hours at a time."

"Yes, Miss Camelia. I think I know. Romeo works that area. Yeah, I know him." Silas beamed a big smile.

"Good, Silas. I'm going to write a letter to my Rosalia, and I trust you'll get it to her. I have to know if she's happy. She's holed up in that convent no better than a prisoner."

"I'll try. I'll try, Miss Camelia."

"Don't just try. You, of all people, have a very special reason to make sure that she's well and happy."

Silas stared at her blankly.

"She's your sister, Silas."

"My sistah? I ain't got no sistah."

"Yes, you do. Rufus Baillieux was your natural daddy, and he was also natural daddy to my Rosalia. That makes you brother and sister." She nodded and looked at him squarely.

"Well, I'll be." He shook his head, dumbfounded, the whites of his eyes poking through the soot on his face and eyelids. "I got a sistah, you say?" Silas lifted his stovepipe hat and scratched his head under his woolly cap.

"You go finish up, Silas, and I'll dash off a letter to my baby girl quick like."

Camelia rushed to her writing table in her boudoir. Now that she knew that Silas's father was Rufus, her third husband, she felt an unusual closeness to the young man.

My Dearest Daughter,

My life is not the same without my little girl. We have never been separated, and I can't bear to think you may be unhappy. I did not get a good feeling from the Mother Superior. Please, *chere,* write a note on the other side of this letter. Tell me if you're happy or miserable. Give it back to Silas. He will wait for it and bring it to me. I trust the dear boy. He has become like a son to me.

I pray every day that you are well.

With all my love,
Mere

Silas and Romeo were on their way to the Holy Family Convent in Romeo's one horse carriage.

"She says she's ma sistah. I never knew I had no sistah."

"Aw, maybe she just sayin' it so you go to the convent."

Silas scratched his head. "I don't think that lady has the disposition to lie. She was married to my natural daddy at one time and had this little girl a hers she's always jawin' about."

As they neared the convent, Silas wondered how he would give Rosalia the letter. "Those nuns don't know me from Adam. Mebbe they slam the doow in ma face."

"They know me. I'll go to the front door and ask them if they want da chimneys sweeped, and you go 'round the back way to the kitchen. There's all the time those young girls in the back in black dresses doin' dishes and peelin' potatoes. Then, they'll slam the front doow and tell me to go 'round to the back. By the time they tell the Mother Lady I'm in the back, you get your business done."

"I don't know how I got myself in this fix," Silas said, frowning. "How I'm gonna know Rosalia? I don't 'member what she looked like. Huh? Tell me that."

"You sure dumb. Just ask the young girl in a black dress with no hair to give the letter to Rosalia, Dummy."

They jumped off the wagon, and Romeo pointed the back way to Silas. "Get going and jest do it! Don't stand there lookin' at me all bug-eyed," Romeo yelled.

Silas knocked on the back door with an apprehensive heart. A young quadroon girl with closely cropped hair in a black dress answered. She looked up directly at Silas.

"Afternoon, ma'm. Could you please give this letter to Rosalia?"

The young postulant shook her head. "Oh, we can't get..."

"I'm Rosalia." Rosalia rushed to the door. "Is it from my mother?" Her voice rose in excitement at the prospect of a letter from a loved one.

"Sure is." Silas smiled with a feeling of relief.

"Is my mother well?"

"Oh, yeah, she's all right, jest bawls for you all the time, but I expect she's well."

"Thank you, Silas." Rosalia heard the Mother Superior coming down the hall and saw her steady gait through the half-opened kitchen door. She slid the letter into her apron pocket and got back to her station. She waved Silas to leave.

She mouthed the words "thank you" to him.

He wasn't sure what she was saying but legged from the convent as fast as he could.

"Miss Camelia said to wait and go back for a letter. How'd I get into this mess anyways?" Silas looked at Romeo for an answer.

"Just wait here a spell. Better than havin' to go back tomorrow." Romeo took out a pocketknife and started to clean his fingernails.

"All of a sudden, I got a sistah. Makes no sense. How come I never knew I had a sistah?"

"Oh, stop your jawin'. I gotta go. I'll come back for you later," Romeo said.

Silas knocked on the back door to find Rosalia, teary-eyed.

She reached out to hand him a letter. "Here," she said. "Now, go."

Dearest Mamma,

I miss you so. I fear that I've made a terrible mistake. I tried to talk to Sister Reginald about leaving the convent. She won't hear of it. I have to wait until after the three-month adjustment period. I'm miserable to think I have to stay here.

I fear that Elmo will never forgive me for hurting him. I know that I love him.

Please help me, Mamma. I'm desperate to come home.

Love,
Rosalia

Chapter 8

"Camelia! This is a rare day when you come to my home. Do come in." Lily's face glowed with pleasure, as her friend entered.

"Lily, I'm so upset. My poor daughter is miserable in that convent, and I'm not sure what to do."

"How do you know, Camelia?"

"I got Silas to sneak a letter to her and she wrote back. She's in a terrible way."

"Oh, dear. That is a shame. Would you like a nice, hot cup of coffee, *chere?* I'll ask Delphine to brew a pot."

"No, thank you, Lily. I can no longer refresh myself in the waters of my memories. I miss my Rosalia so much I can hardly bear the loneliness without her. The house seems empty. I pray she'll find a way to leave the convent and come home to me. Am I sinning to want her to leave the convent?"

"Lord knows, no, Camelia. You love your child. Anything that natural cannot be a sin."

"Are you sure?" Camelia asked through a sob. "I need you to reassure me, Lily, that I'm not sinning by wanting my girl back home."

"My dear, sweet friend. I know how much you love your daughter. How can that be a sin, to love?"

"Oh, you make me feel so much better, Lily. I need to decide how I'll get my daughter out of her miserable situation." Camelia sighed. "How is Elmo doing these days? Any better?"

"He doesn't appear to be happy. Mostly keeps to himself." Lily lowered her eyes, as she spoke of her son.

"Lily, my dear girl says she loves Elmo in her letter. I had my doubts, but at least that's one good thing. She loves him."

"Oh, I'm so happy that she loves my son. I feared there was no love. Are you sure, Camelia?"

"I know my daughter. She never would have said she loves him if she didn't. Is Elmo in? May I speak to him?"

"He stays in the *garconniere*. Let me take you to him."

"Lily, may I speak to him privately? I have something to tell him, a most delicate subject for his ears only."

"Of course, *chere*. I'll take you down the hall. If you need me later, I'll be in the solarium."

Lily accompanied Camelia down the center hall and opened the door to the courtyard. Camelia walked across the courtyard and climbed the squeaky stairs to Elmo's rooms. She knocked rather meekly, wondering if she was doing the right thing.

"Madame Arceneaux?" Elmo looked perplexed when he saw Camelia in the doorway. "Do come in."

She entered a room that looked sparse compared to Lily's grandiose home. There was little furniture except for a wooden table and chairs at the window and some comfortable wing chairs for reading. A bookcase lined one wall. "I hope I'm not intruding, Elmo."

"No. Not at all." He gestured for her to sit in a comfortable chair.

"Elmo, I've known you since you were a young boy in short pants. I trust your judgment, and I think you've known me well enough to trust mine."

He paced the room with his arms behind his back and did not speak.

"I know that my daughter has hurt you, and you feel betrayed, but it wasn't because she does not love you."

He turned to look at her with a hardened stare. "How can you honestly say that?"

"I snuck a letter to her at the convent. She returned with a note saying she had made a terrible mistake by going into the religious life. She wants to leave, but the Mother Superior will not hear of it. She is being held like a prisoner."

"Isn't that what she wanted? She said she had prayed about it for a long time. And all the while, I was courting her." His bitter voice was as defeated as his posture.

"Oh, dear Elmo. Please listen. She said in her letter that she loves you."

"That is hard to believe considering that she left me when we were making plans to be married." He walked to the window with a faraway look, his back to her.

"Elmo, please look at me. I want to explain to you why she did that. I wanted to forget the unfortunate thing that happened in her life, but I feel I must tell you so that you will understand Rosalia better. Something happened to her long before she started seeing you. Then, I was so happy when you courted her. She always came home, looking so hopeful."

"Why wouldn't she have hope?" he asked, his voice gruff from the still-fresh memories of the two of them together.

"She was so unhappy before you. Oh, you don't know what she went through."

"What made her so unhappy? What aren't you telling me?"

"I can hardly breathe the words. Oh, Rosalia would rather die than I give away her awful secret."

"I want to know. What happened?" He turned around sharply to face her.

"Will you promise not to mention it to Rosalia or to anyone—not even your mother? Rosalia would absolutely die if anyone knew."

He stood in silence, his arms folded in front of him.

"Please, Elmo, tell me that I can trust you not to repeat what I am about to tell you either to Rosalia or to anyone."

"You can trust me, madame. I will not breathe the secret to anyone."

Camelia let out a sob. "I'm sorry. I can barely think of that dreadful day without falling apart. I remember the day when I came home from hanging drapes at Katia's flat. Rosalia was sitting in a tub of cold water in the kitchen trying to get Rufus's smell off of her body. She kept scrubbing until her skin was raw. When I went into her room, I saw the blood on her duvet. He stole my baby's virginity. Oh, I never knew a daddy could do that to his little girl." Camelia bawled in her handkerchief. "She does not speak of it, but we both know what happened. I'm sure of it. She does not feel worthy to be your wife, Elmo, because she feels like a tainted woman."

He clenched his fists. "Oh, God, I never thought of my innocent Rosalia in that light." He bent low to hide his grief and misting eyes. He swiped his eyes and stood to face her.

Camelia's heart swelled when she beheld Elmo's solemn face. "She was always happy when she came home after seeing you. I saw it in her expression. When she talked about you, she was always happy. I was so elated that she finally met someone that she felt so comfortable with."

"Do you feel she will still want to marry me?"

"Oh, yes, Elmo. However, you will have to take it very slow in the bedroom. Never force yourself on her. Let her come to you. She will come around. I know she will. It may take a little time, but she will come to you. She loves you." Camelia's memory turned to the convent. "Oh, we have to get her out of that prison."

"I felt she thought of that place as an oasis, a place away from me."

"Oh, no, Elmo. Never think those thoughts again. Here, I brought her note." She walked to the table. "Come here to the table and read it."

Elmo sat at the small table and unfolded Rosalia's note, accidently ripping the paper between his nervous fingers.

"See here, Elmo, she is worried that you will not forgive her. She says she loves you. See." She pointed to the words.

He glanced across the table at Camelia. "Shall we go to the convent and bring her home?"

"Oh, yes, my future *gendre.*"

Few words were spoken between Camelia and Elmo on the way to the convent. As they approached Orleans Street, Elmo asked, "Do you want me to come in with you?"

"Yes, Elmo. I don't know what to expect. This Mother Superior is very hard to reason with. She only recites rules."

When the carriage came to a stop, Camelia looked up to the building as an imposing fortress meant to keep everyone in the world out. The coachman helped Camelia step down from the carriage and opened the iron gates. She walked to the door with a heavy heart.

A knock on the door summoned a postulant. "Yes, madame?"

"Madame Arceneaux calling for Rosalia Baillieux."

"We are not allowed visitors, madame."

"This is not a visit. I must come in for my daughter."

Camelia set her foot on the threshold and made her way inside. Elmo followed.

The postulant eyed Elmo with a worried look, as if she had never seen a man enter the convent. "This is most unusual, madame."

"Can you tell me where Rosalia is?" Camelia asked.

Sister Reginald appeared in the large foyer. She spied Camelia and then looked toward Elmo. "What is the meaning of this? You know the rules!"

"Yes, I quite know your rules, Sister. I am here for my daughter, Rosalia Baillieux."

"She can't leave now. I explained that to you. The rules are…"

Camelia walked past the nun and called out, "Rosalia!"

She turned to Elmo. "You go that way and I'll go this way."

"You can't go there. This is a convent!" Sister Reginald screamed.

"Rosalia!" Camelia yelled, as she turned to the left corridor, leading to the kitchen where two young girls were peeling potatoes. "Is Rosalia in here?"

"No, madame," a postulant looked up and answered.

Camelia ran back in the hallway and entered the stairway. Sister Reginald followed, screaming at the top of her lungs. "Stop this intrusion. Madame, you cannot go up there. That is where the postulants sleep."

"I've seen girls sleep before. There's nothing mysterious about that." Camelia hurried up the stairs.

"Really! What do you want, madame?"

"I want my daughter." Camelia opened each door to look inside. As she peeked into a room, two postulants were praying on their knees.

She descended the stairs and ran to the other side of the building, the nun following. Camelia opened another door. Three postulants peered up from the books they were reading. "Is Rosalia in here?"

"No, madame," they answered.

"Do you know where she is? I am her mother."

"Yes, madame. She went to the chapel to replace the votive candles," a young postulant, Anna, said.

"Will you show me where the chapel is?" Camelia asked.

"You needn't show her!" Sister Reginald spoke sternly.

"I will show you. She cries herself to sleep every night for you," Anna said.

The young girl rose and led Camelia through the hall past several rooms. They heard the chorus of girls' voices chanting through a door before coming to the chapel.

As they entered the chapel, Elmo walked swiftly toward them. "I haven't found Rosalia."

They found Rosalia lighting candles on the altar. "Rosalia, my sweet daughter," Camelia cried.

Rosalia turned in surprise. "Mamma. Elmo. I was just praying for a miracle, and here you are."

Elmo rushed toward Rosalia. "*Ma Cherie*, are you all right? Your mother said you were very unhappy."

"This is most unusual. What is he doing here?" Sister Reginald demanded, wrinkling up her nose.

"He is here to take her home," Camelia said.

The old nun's face grayed, as she threatened Anna, shaking a finger at her. "You will pay for this."

Anna looked frightened.

"Do you want to come home with us, *chere?*" Camelia asked.

"Oh, yes. I want to leave, too. Will you take me home?"

Camelia wrapped an arm around the young girl. "Of course, *chere*. You don't have to stay here if you don't want to."

Anna smiled in relief.

"Come, Daughter, we're taking you home."

Elmo led Rosalia to her mother upon leaving the chapel.

"I've never, in my fifty-five years in the convent witnessed such an outlandish sight. A man in the convent! Taking two postulants out! Why, I've never!" The old nun walked alongside Rosalia and Anna. She craned to see them, as she had difficulty keeping up with them. "You know the rules! Why are you doing this?"

"Let's leave as quickly as we can, *chere,*" Camelia said.

Rosalia hesitated remembering something she left upstairs. "Oh, there was one thing, my daily missal. Can I go up to get it?" She looked at her mother for approval.

"You can't take things out of the convent. That should go to the postulants who are entering. It's for the church," Sister Reginald said.

"Mamma, you bought me that missal for my confirmation. I do love it."

"Never mind, *chere.* I'll buy you another one. I don't want to delay getting you girls home."

The old nun was iced with shock, as Camelia and the young girls ignored her authority. "You can't leave just like that," Sister Reginald said. "Come into my office, and we'll discuss this."

The nun's orders did not discourage Camelia's intentions of getting Rosalia out of the convent. They only encouraged her to ignore any more delays the nun might create.

Sister Reginald's wrinkled face dropped, as Elmo took Rosalia's hand and led her out of the convent. Camelia followed with her arm around Anna.

The relieved look in her daughter's face made Camelia feel happy, as she sat across from her in the carriage. She comforted the young girl, Anna, who sat next to her. "You'll be home safe and sound soon, *chere.*"

"I didn't think I'd ever get to come home again," Anna said.

"And why not? I'm sure that your mother will be elated to see you, as I am to see Rosalia."

Camelia looked out of the carriage window to give Rosalia and Elmo the tiniest bit of privacy.

Elmo put an arm around Rosalia and studied her eyes. "Did you miss me?"

"Oh, yes, I did. And did you miss me?" she asked.

"More than I can ever tell you. I've lived a lonely life since you left."

"I'm sorry. I thought it would be better for you. I don't know why..."

"I know." He put his head next to hers and held her hand. "It will be okay now, *chere*. As long as you're near me, everything will be okay. I never want to be away from you again."

"I never want to be away from you again either, Elmo."

"Then, does that mean you'll marry me?"

She could hear her heart thump, as he squeezed her hand. "Yes, that means I'll marry you."

Chapter 9

It was to be a simple, family wedding. Rosalia wanted to be married in one of Camelia's old wedding dresses, but Camelia insisted on sewing her daughter a new gown made especially for her tiny figure.

She looked lovely in a white silk gown with lace from breast line to the high neck and her sister's honitan lace veil trimmed shorter, since Rosalia's gown bore no train. The white satin orange blossoms that Collette wore on her wedding day adorned Rosalia's head.

Raymone, Rosalia's cousin, walked Rosalia down the white-carpeted wedding aisle at the evening candlelit wedding ceremony on a Thursday night. Collette and Dominique were proud to be their main witnesses.

Camelia cried tears of joy during the wedding ceremony, as the couple promised to love, honor, and obey. She talked to her late fourth husband during the ceremony. "Claudio, I will be without my baby, Rosalia. I will need you more than ever now."

Her sisters, nieces, and nephews were used to these conversations that Camelia had with Claudio. It seemed to pacify her during stressful moments. They accepted her dead husband as part of the family.

Afterward, the family went to Lily's home for the reception. Camelia had La Fonda and Andre's children with her, but Andre's family did not know that these were Andre's children. As far as they knew, they were La Fonda's children, and Camelia was taking care of them while their mother was in a tuberculosis sanitarium. They also thought that Andre was still at St. Maurice's Parish across town and couldn't get away from his responsibilities. Camelia couldn't bear to tell her sister, Alma, the truth. She thought it would break her heart.

Elmo looked handsome in his black, double-breasted tailcoat and couldn't keep his eyes off his bride. They danced the first dance of the evening, as the family watched the young couple.

They took a break from dancing to go to the second parlor to take wedding photographs. The little picture man, Bellocq, was setting up his camera, and soon had Collette, Dominique, Rosalia, and Elmo in position to take a formal photograph. Elmo admired his wife adoringly.

"Please, monsieur, do not look at your wife. Look into the camera and smile. And madame, tilt your head the tiniest bit toward your husband."

The newly wedded couple laughed in sheer joy at hearing the new words "your wife" and "your husband."

"No, that was too much," the photographer said.

"Just a small smile, not a laugh."

After the formal photographs were taken, Rosalia gave her bridal bouquet to her mother to take to the sisters at St. Mary's Convent, as was the custom.

Elmo and Rosalia heard the music floating from the solarium and soon joined the wedding guests. Elmo danced with his mother, mother-in-law, and sister-in-law, and then returned to his bride. "Did I tell you how much I love you today, *ma cherie?*"

"No, I don't believe you did, my husband."

"I love you with all my heart."

"I love you too, sweet husband. I pray that I will not disappoint you."

"You will never disappoint me, *cherie.*"

It would be an embarrassment for a creole couple to stay to the end of their wedding reception. Custom was for the bride and groom to spend the first days after the wedding in the bride's home, but since Camelia's rooms were filled with her nephew's children, Rosalia and Elmo decided to stay in Lily's home. Lily was delighted with her son's marriage and invited the couple to live with her.

Elmo and Rosalia quietly left the solarium to Elmo's *garconniere.* When they entered the boudoir, Rosalia saw that her mother had placed a beautiful nightgown and peignoir on the bed.

"I will give you some privacy, *chere.* Do you want me to unbutton your gown before I leave?" He looked at her with reverence.

"Maybe you can just unbutton the buttons back here and then leave?" She held her arm back, pointing to the top buttons of her gown.

"Of course, *chere*." He gently unbuttoned the top buttons of her gown and wanted to rub his hand against her smooth light brown skin. *Would she panic if I merely rubbed the skin across her back and traveled to her beautifully shaped breasts?*

His fingers slowly unbuttoned the last two silky buttons to her waist. As he lifted her hair, he kissed the nape of her neck. He hesitated. She stood still with her back to him.

"When you want me, my sweet wife, call for me. I'll be in the next room."

"Oui," she spoke in a trembling voice. When he was out of sight, she went behind a dressing screen and stepped out of her wedding gown and placed it on the chaise longue. She put on her nightgown and admired the tiny stitches her mother had delicately sewn, then covered the nightgown with the peignoir.

"Elmo, you can come in now," she called out in a cracked voice.

He entered with adoring eyes fastened on her. "You look beautiful my sweetheart. I have some pajamas here my mother gave me for this special occasion. I will change into them."

She turned her back to him and walked to the window.

"Why don't you sit on the bed while I change?" he asked.

"That's okay. I'll just look at the stars."

After he changed quickly, he walked behind her, holding her around her waist. "It's a beautiful night, isn't it?"

"Yes, quite."

"This is our first night together. We will have a good life together, won't we?"

"Yes, we will."

He heard uncertainty in her voice and picked her up, placing her on the bed. She scooted under the duvet.

"Don't you want to take your peignoir off?"

"No."

"Can I take it off for you?"

"No, I'm quite comfortable with it on."

He leaned over for a kiss. She stared at the ceiling.

"Are you tired, my sweetheart?" he asked.

"Yes, I am quite tired."

As he initiated a long kiss, they heard singing outside in the courtyard. Elmo's friends were serenading them. He joined her under the duvet.

Usually, a newly wedded couple made love while their friends serenaded them. That night, the newly wedded couple lay side-by-side, not buck-naked, but fully covered with nightclothes under a duvet, simply holding hands.

La Fonda

Chapter 10

Scrubbing a stain on a tablecloth over a washboard in a laundry tub, La Fonda appeared distracted. She changed her stance to stop and cough.

Camelia looked across at La Fonda, rubbing on the washboard in an even tempo. "Why don't you stop and take a rest?"

"I've got to finish washing this tablecloth."

"No, you just stop now. You've been working too hard lately. I've noticed how tired you've been looking. I never see you have any fun. You and Andre should go dancing some time."

"Dancing? Why, I've never gone dancing in my whole life."

"That's just it. You should go some time."

"And who's supposed to watch my three children when I go about dancing?"

"I'd be happy to keep them for the night so that you and Andre can have a night out."

"I don't even have a dress to go dancing in and never have." She looked at Camelia. "Uh oh. I just know when I see you smile at me like that, you're up to no good."

"Mercy, I've got scads of extra material lyin' around. I can put together a dress for you in no time. Wouldn't take much fabric to sew one for you. Come into my boudoir, La Fonda. Pick out something you'd like. Come on," she urged.

She wiped her hands, and reluctantly followed Camelia into her boudoir. Camelia already had large swatches of material laid out on the duvet of her four-poster bed. Remnants ranged in colors from yellows and oranges to pinks and lilacs to purples to every shade of blue.

"Hold your favorite color against you, La Fonda, and let's see how it looks on you."

La Fonda marveled at the beautiful fabrics. She couldn't resist lifting a piece of French blue material from the duvet and admiring it. She held it against herself and looked down upon it. Tears almost came to La Fonda's eyes, as she admired the blue material and daintily smoothed her hand across it. She became overwhelmed, and looked across the room toward Camelia.

Camelia saw the look in La Fonda's eyes and knew she had her. "Come into the front hallway here, and look at yourself in the petticoat looking glass," Camelia said, as she walked out of her boudoir. La Fonda followed her, and when she saw herself in the looking glass, she could imagine herself, looking fresh and pretty in the beautiful dress Camelia would sew for her. In that moment, she no longer remembered a reason not to go dancing.

La Fonda sauntered into Camelia's kitchen dressed in her new French blue dress.

"You look drop dead gorgeous, La Fonda. That dress sure looks good on you. And your hair looks so nice with those little wisps combed toward your pretty face."

"Much obliged, Miss Camelia. You sure made me a pretty dress I've never had the likes of," La Fonda said in a toneless voice, gazing at the floor.

"What's the matter?" Camelia arched her eyebrows.

"Well, I knew this was gonna happen. I'm all dolled up for nothin'. Andre's not home yet and it's eight o'clock, and I know just as I'm standin' here, he's not gonna come home 'til we're all sleepin'."

Camelia shook her head. "Oh, no. Don't say that. He'll be here."

"No, Miss Camelia. He's working for that crabby butcher tonight, and he never comes home early when he works for him. It's always after we're sound asleep."

"Well, not tonight. He's coming home, and you're going dancing. I fed the children. They're playing in the boudoir. See that they're tucked in bed. I'm bringing Andre home. You can bet on it."

Camelia rushed through the dark streets of *Faubourg Marigny,* dreading to confront Maximelian Parmenter.

He didn't get much respect from his customers, so he made the most of his importance from being the owner of the butcher shop.

The store was dark. She tried the door anyway. To her relief, it opened onto a dark, cold shop with a dim light from two candles off in a corner.

A raspy voice called out. "We're closed. Can't you see that?"

Looking over the counter toward the candlelight, her eyes shot to his fat workingman's hands marked with blood and then his bloody apron.

"I'm not here to buy meat. I've come for Andre."

"Don't you know he's working? You can't just come in here for Andre. We work hard here. How do you think I got this business?'

She let out a mocking laugh. "Oh, come on now, Max. We all know you got this here meat market from your wife's inheritance. And then after she bought you this place, you left her for another woman." She walked the length of the counter, hanging onto it in the darkness, into the freezing, barn-like back room where hindquarters of cows and pigs hung from the high ceiling.

"You can't go back there to bother him."

Camelia ignored the butcher and looked up to Andre, chopping meat in a loft by the light of a kerosene lamp.

"Andre, don't you know what day this is? It must be half past eight by now. Your poor wife is waiting for you."

He peered down from the loft. "I didn't know it was that late. Time got away from me. I haven't finished here."

"You've been here all day since dawn. It's time for you to leave this godforsaken place."

The butcher's eyes filled with fury. "He can't leave! Can't you see he has work to do?"

"There's always work to do. He's to come home."

Max swayed in anger, puffed, and put his fat hands on his burly hips. "Says who?"

"I say. That's who!" Camelia's voice rang louder.

"You don't count here, woman. This is my butcher shop. And I'm the boss." He pointed to his chest. "And who are you?" He sneered and blew a haughty breath.

Unruffled, she spat back at him. "I'm the woman who, since you were a tyke, always sews extra wide seams in the seat of your pants so you could wear your diapers. That's who. Remember?" She pointed to her chest and gave him a spirited nod.

She looked up to Andre. "You promised La Fonda you'd take her dancing. Get down from up there and come home. Now!"

Max looked perplexed, first at her, then up at Andre. "You're not going to listen to her, are you?"

Andre wiped the blood from his hands and threw off his long, white bloodstained coat. He came down the ladder at a fast clip and joined his aunt. They left arm in arm.

❧

Camelia had arranged for Silas to drive La Fonda and Andre to the *Boucher's* Dance. "Let me help you, madame." Silas extended an arm and helped La Fonda into his one horse wagon.

"Why thank you much, Silas." La Fonda felt like a queen, grinning from ear to ear.

Andre joined her and took her hand in his.

She looked down at Andre's caramel-colored hand over hers with his perfectly trimmed fingernails, white half-moons showing through. Then, she saw her scrub worn hands, the hands of a washerwoman, dark and rough. A sudden twinge of self-pity came over her. She wondered why Andre loved her, a poor, black girl. But then, he gave her that look full of love, and she felt beautiful and secure in the French blue dress Camelia had sewed for her, so that she could feel like a young girl in love.

At the dance, Andre led La Fonda to a bench along the wall. "La Fonda, I wanted to give this little gift to you when we were alone." He handed her a tiny, velvet box. "Open it."

She opened the box to find gold earrings. "Oh, my goodness, Andre. Are these earrings? I've never had earrings before in my whole life. Can we afford them?"

"I worked all week and had a little extra. You deserve them, *cherie*. Put them on."

"Oh, they have little wires on them."

"Aren't your ears pierced?"

"No. Do they need to be pierced?"

"Yes," he said through a laugh. "I'm sure *Tante* Camelia will be happy to pierce them."

"Oh, I don't know about that."

"Don't fret, my love. Let's just enjoy the evening. We'll worry about that tomorrow."

He led her to the dance floor. "Don't be nervous, *chere*. Just follow me."

"But Andre, I've never danced before."

"You've watched people at fetes where you worked, haven't you?"

"Yes, but I never danced."

He held her close to his body, as he always imagined he would and led her. "One, two. One, two. See? You can count to two, can't you, La Fonda?"

"I guess so. Where'd you learn to dance?"

"My family always had fetes in our home. My cousins danced with me, as soon as I learned to walk."

Soon, she relaxed and learned to follow him. He twirled her around, and she quickly came back to him in a warm embrace. She started to enjoy dancing with Andre. A big smile crossed over her face.

"I love you, La Fonda."

"I love you, Andre. You make my life like heaven."

"After years in a prison of loneliness, I almost didn't come to you and the children. I dread to think how empty my life would have been without you. I'd be living with that old priest, not feeling anything. Please forgive me for not leaving my old life sooner and coming to you."

She nodded in acceptance. "I understand, Andre. You wanted to keep your vows."

He saw a light of joy in her eyes, grateful for these few moments of happiness.

"Look what Andre gave me last night. Earrings! Can you imagine me wearing gold earrings on my ears, Miss Camelia?" She extended her hand, holding the opened box.

"Oh, I see. They're beautiful, La Fonda."

Camelia went to get her little black bag. La Fonda busied herself with hand washing some bloomers in a washtub. She rubbed lightly on the washboard in pitter-patter fashion.

She saw Camelia pull something out of her black bag and put it under the fire on the stove. "What is that you have there, Miss Camelia?"

"It's just a needle."

"A what? For what?"

"Sit down here, La Fonda. I'll pierce your ears."

"Oh, no. You're not putting that needle in my ears."

"Come on now. Don't be a baby. You want to wear those beautiful earrings that Andre got for you, don't you?"

"I'll just look at them in the pretty little box. It's the thought that counts. Isn't that what you always say?"

"Come on, now, La Fonda. You're a mother. You had three babies. This is just a little prick in the ear."

Camelia pulled La Fonda by the arm into a chair. "Sit. I'll clean your ears off with this alcohol first. There now, that didn't hurt, did it?"

La Fonda shook her head.

La Fonda tightened her lips and grimaced, as Camelia stuck a needle in her ear. Camelia's nimble fingers immediately placed a gold earring in the lobe. "There now. That wasn't so bad, was it?"

La Fonda sat frozen with her eyes shut. "You don't need to do the other one, do you?"

With that, Camelia pierced the other ear and put the earring in place.

"Done! See how easy that was? Camelia suddenly looked into La Fonda's watery eyes and felt her forehead. "You feel hot. Are you okay?"

La Fonda leaned over and coughed. "Yes. I just have a little cough."

"You can hardly speak with all your coughing fits."

La Fonda ran to the petticoat looking glass in the front hallway. "Oh, look, Miss Camelia. Aren't they beauties? I'm never going to take them off."

"See. I told you that it wouldn't be so bad."

La Fonda hurried to the kitchen to resume her work.

"Tell me what you did at the dance, La Fonda."

Her eyes lit, as she spoke. "Oh, I learned a dance from Andre last night, the two-step. Here, let me show you."

She wiped her hands, grabbed Camelia, and put her arms around her like a man. "Like this, Miss Camelia, One, two, one two. You can count to one, two, can't you?" And they trotted around Camelia's kitchen.

They sidled together, as La Fonda sang out to Camelia. She added a trill to the words.

Won't you come home, Bill Bailey, won't you
come home
I moan the whole night long
I'll do the cookin' honey, I'll pay the rent
I know I done you wrong
Remember that rainy evenin'
I drove you out with nothin' but a fine-tooth
comb

"This is wonderful, *chere*. Just dandy," Camelia
said.

"Oh! I just love this. Oops. I almost fell. It's been
so long since I've danced. I just adore dancing to
happy music."

"We danced like this, Miss Camelia. It was just
like heaven when he held me close. She whirled
Camelia around the kitchen, laughing, and suddenly
let out a wheezing cough, as blood spurted from her
mouth onto Camelia's dress. "Oh, I'm so sorry. I
don't know what happened."

"*Mon Dieu*. You are coughing blood. That is not
good. Come. You must lie down."

"No, I don't need to lie down. I've got to finish
this laundry." She coughed again and couldn't stop.

"Come with me, La Fonda. I know a sick person
when I see one. I'll fix the day bed in my room so you
can rest."

Camelia urged her to her boudoir where she pulled
out a folded bed in an alcove in her room, unfolded it,
and put clean sheets on it. "Come and lie down."

"Do you have a handkerchief, Miss Camelia?"

She pulled a handkerchief from the bottom armoire drawer and handed it to La Fonda, who held it to her mouth to hide more blood.

"Funny thing. I feel cold now. Do you have a quilt?" La Fonda shivered, as she rubbed her arms with her hands.

As La Fonda lay on the small bed, Camelia covered her. "You must rest, La Fonda. I think this calls for a doctor. I'll be back as soon as I can." *Oh, dear God in Heaven, let it not be what I think it is.*

La Fonda appeared groggy when the doctor approached her. Camelia placed a gentle hand on La Fonda's arm to reassure her. "The doctor's just going to ask you some questions."

The doctor looked into her weary eyes. "Madame, please sit up. Are you tired?"

"Yes. Powerful tired."

He spotted blood on her dress, and pulled out a stethoscope from his black bag. He applied it to her chest. "Please take a breath. Breathe in. Breathe out."

La Fonda's frightened eyes followed his motions. She wheezed a cough and spit up blood in the handkerchief.

"Do you cough often?"

"Oh, well, I do cough a spell now and then."

"And do you always cough up blood?"

"Been happenin' lately."

"You also appear to have a fever." He looked up at Camelia, standing next to him. "This poor girl has been suffering from tuberculosis and malnutrition. She needs immediate rest. She should be taken to the tuberculosis ward at Charity Hospital. I have another patient that I will be taking there this afternoon. I can take Madame Delacroixe in my carriage when I take my other patient."

"Does she have to go today? It's so sudden." Camelia looked down at La Fonda with pity.

The doctor nodded with a serious expression. "I must go to the sanitarium today. They are expecting me. I probably won't be going again after today for a spell. And my other tuberculosis patient must go today. They have prepared a bed for her. She is very ill."

"Where does he want to take me?" La Fonda looked up at Camelia with pleading eyes. "I can't leave my children."

"The doctor wants to take you to a hospital, where you can rest, *chere*. They will take care of you so that you can get well. You are sick."

"I can't go today. I didn't even finish my work," La Fonda said. "And Andre. I have to talk to Andre about it."

"I'll go out and ask Gossie to go to the Butcher Shop and get Andre to come home. Gossie is playing outside."

"Oh yes, please get Andre. Please!" Tears came to La Fonda's eyes, and she brushed them away.

The doctor looked down at La Fonda. "Madame, don't be alarmed. We will take good care of you. Perhaps you have been working too hard. You will get to rest and get the best medicines. Then, when you're well, you can come home."

"But I don't want to go until I talk to Andre."

The doctor rose and turned to Camelia. He looked at his gold pocket watch. "I will pick up my other patient and be back in forty-five minutes to take Madame Delacroixe to the sanitarium. Please have her ready."

Camelia walked the doctor to the front door. He turned to her before leaving. "This young woman is very sick. If she is not confined to a sanitarium for complete bed rest, she will not live to raise her three children. You have no choice, madame, but to send her to the sanitarium today."

"I hate to be the one to decide to send her," Camelia said with trepidation.

"Would you rather have her life on your conscience, madame?"

"Oh, mercy, no. I want for this child to live. To me, she is but a child, raising children. She has never had family to love her, being an orphan. I want for her to live, not just for me, but for her children and for my nephew, who needs her."

"Then, have her ready to leave when I call for her. *Bonjour.*"

Camelia hurried down her front steps to find Gossie. When she spotted him, she called out to him. "Gossie, run to the butcher shop and tell your father to come home as soon as he can. Tell him that *Tante* Camelia wants him."

"Yes, *Tante.*"

Gossie ran as fast as he could, his crippled leg holding him back a bit. When he reached the butcher shop, he asked Monsieur Parmenter, "May I please talk to my father?"

"He is in the back and he is very busy. Don't keep him from his work."

When Gossie ran in the back room, he saw his father in the midst of bloody hogs' feet and hindquarters. His father's bloody hands, slashed at a bulk of flesh. "Father, *Tante* Camelia wants you to come home as soon as you can."

Andre smiled at the sight of his son. "Do you know what it's about?"

"No, Father."

Monsieur Parmenter rushed into the slaughter room. "I told you, boy, not to keep him from his work."

"It seems I'm wanted at home," Andre said.

"You know damn well you've got to slaughter these hogs today so we can drain them during the night and have them ready for tomorrow's pig roast. You don't leave now, Man."

"Yes, you're right, Monsieur Parmenter. I'll get the hogs slaughtered." He turned to his son. "Gossie, tell *Tante* Camelia that I can't leave right now. I'll be home just as soon as I finish my work. Can you remember that?"

"Yes, Father." Gossie wanted to get closer to his father for a hug or a touch, but a glance at his father's bloody hands and apron drove him out of the freezing room that reeked of pig flesh.

Chapter 11

A hot breeze hit Camelia in the face, as she rushed down the stairs of La Fonda's back attic flat. She hurried past the courtyard and ran to her front flat. Upon entering her boudoir, she bent over La Fonda, resting on the daybed.

"La Fonda, I've gone to your flat to get some of your things. I packed some clean bloomers, some other underwear you might need, a tooth brush, tooth powder, and a sweater in case you get cold and a pair of slippers. I threw a comb in there, too. And I put a nice nightgown in there just in case you may need it."

Squinting up at Camelia, La Fonda said, "I don't want to go to no hospital."

"I know, *chere*, but you're sick, and the doctor said you need to go to get well. You want to get over this terrible cough, don't you?"

"I want to talk to Andre."

"I sent Gossie to get Andre. He should be here soon."

Tears clouded La Fonda's eyes. "I'm scared to leave here. This is the only home I've ever known. It's not fancy, but it's my home, and you and Andre and the children are all I have in the world. If I'm away from you, I'm all alone just like I was before I met Andre. I'm scared to death I'll never see you again."

"I'll come visit you in the hospital. You know that. And Andre will come to visit you, too."

"And the children, too? I can't live without my children. And Baby Blossom is so little. She'll think I left her. Oh, Miss Camelia, will you take care of her for me?"

"Of course, I'll take care of her, and I'll take care of Gossie and Geetie, too. You know, La Fonda, Andre has always been my favorite nephew. I'll take extra special care of his children."

"I never even got around to getting Gossie in school. Oh, I wasn't a good mother, was I?"

"You're a wonderful mother, La Fonda, and I'll try as hard as I can to be a mother to them, too. Now, I think I've got everything you'll need right away in this burlap bag. They'll have soap and towels at the hospital."

"I'm cold again. I get hot, and now I'm cold." La Fonda's teeth chattered, as she huddled under the quilt.

"You must sit up, *chere*. I know you're tired, but we've got to put a clean dress on you. That one's a bit messed up. Lift your arms." Camelia slipped a clean dress over La Fonda's head. "Thattagirl. You're doing fine."

Camelia heard someone running through the flat. Gossie ran into the room and looked at his mother, shivering. "What's the matter, Mamma? Why are you in that bed?" He turned to Camelia. *"Tante,* Father said he'll come home as soon as he finishes his work. He can't come home now."

"Of all things. Andre can't come home because of that confounded butcher." She looked at Gossie. "Dear Nephew, your mamma is sick. She's going to have to go to the hospital."

"Hospital? Why does she have to go?" Gossie asked with fear in his eyes.

La Fonda peered over the quilt at Gossie, staring back at her. "Come here, child. Give mamma a big hug."

He rushed to his mother and threw himself in her arms.

La Fonda leaned on one elbow. "Son, now I want to tell you something. You have to listen to *Tante* Camelia just like she's your mamma. I have to go to the hospital. I'll come back as soon as I can, but you promise me you'll be good while I'm gone. Promise?"

"I promise," Gossie said, looking down.

"And since you're the oldest in the family, I will depend on you to look after your sisters. You know you're a whole two years older than Geetie. And Blossom is still a baby so she has to be watched. You understand?"

"Yes, Mamma, I understand, but I don't want you to go. When are you coming back?" He started to cry.

"We'll have none of that now. You're a big boy. Act like one," La Fonda said.

When they heard the knock on the door, Camelia gave a look and a nod to La Fonda. She helped her up to a sitting position. "Help your mamma get her shoes on, Gossie."

Gossie knelt on the floor and slipped his mother's shoes on, as he stared up at her, holding back tears. La Fonda's heart swelled, as she beheld the sorrowful look in her son. "You're such a good boy, Gossie. I love you so much I can't even tell you. More than a bushel full. More than a hundred bushels full." She kissed her son tenderly on both cheeks.

"I love you a hundred bushels full, too, Mamma. Will you come back to me soon?" He kissed her lips.

"Yes, I'll come home just as soon as I can."

"Promise?"

"Sure enough. I promise, son."

"Are you cold, La Fonda? I've got a sweater here for you." Camelia scoured the burlap bag.

La Fonda reached for the sweater, and Camelia helped her on with it.

They left the flat and eyed the waiting carriage. Geetie came running up to La Fonda on the banquette with Blossom following when they saw their mother approach the carriage. "Mamma, where are you going?" Geetie asked.

"I'm just going to the hospital for a while, Sugar. You be a good girl and keep an eye on your baby sister."

"No, Mamma. Don't go. I want you to stay here." Geetie grabbed her mother's arm in protest. "Take me with you."

"Child, I can't take you with me. I'll be back. You stay with *Tante* Camelia."

"No! I don't want to stay with *Tante* Camelia. I want you, Mamma." The child screamed in horror.

The doctor opened the carriage door. "Please, madame, we must arrive at the hospital before candlelighting."

Blossom pulled at La Fonda's dress. "Mamma! Mamma!"

La Fonda embraced Camelia, as the carriage door opened.

"Madame, please!" the doctor urged.

The little girls reached for their mother hysterically. La Fonda bent to kiss and embrace them. "You be good girls and listen to *Tante* Camelia."

The coachman helped La Fonda into the carriage. She held in tears, as she watched her crying children through the window, fear in their eyes. She covered her ears to their ghastly cries, but she would still hear their agony for the next several months.

❦

The children were eating dinner at Camelia's kitchen table when Andre walked in. His look of surprise to see his children went unnoticed. "*Bonsoir, Tante.* What is it you wanted?"

"Father!" Gossie was about to get up from the table.

Blossom reached out to Andre from her high chair.

"Not now, children. Finish eating your dinner. I must speak to your father. Andre, come into the dining room."

He failed to hide the worry crinkling around his eyes, as he sat at his aunt's dining table. "Where is La Fonda?"

"Andre, La Fonda is very ill. I called Doctor Broussard in today, because she was coughing up blood with a fever and then chills. I've been noticing she has not been feeling very well of late. My worst fears came true. La Fonda has tuberculosis. The doctor said she must go to the tuberculosis sanitarium immediately for complete bed rest, or she will not live to raise her children."

"And she had to go today?" Andre's incredulous look told her he did not believe her.

"Yes, Andre. I tried to get you to come home to talk to her, and oh, how she wanted to talk to you. But the doctor was going to the sanitarium today and didn't think he would be going for quite a spell. He insisted on taking her today for her health's sake."

Andre leaned forward and put his head in his hands. "What are we going to do without her? She does everything. She works, she takes care of the children, and she takes care of me, too. I don't know if I can live without her, *Tante.*"

"Now is not the time to think about yourself, Nephew. You have three children to think about. You just work like she did when she was without you. And pray that she gets well enough to come back to you."

"I don't know if I can do that."

"You mean to tell me that you're not as strong as she is?"

"No, I guess I'm not."

"Well, you just pray for strength. And be an example to your children. They need you now."

It was one of her busy drape-sewing days. Camelia rushed down her front stairs to look out for the children. She had sent the ten and twelve-year-old girls who lived in her building to take Blossom Rose for ice cream. She saw them coming home in the distance. As she turned the other way, she saw Andre staggering up the street in an awful drunken manner in a wrinkled black suit and dirty collar.

"Evenin', *Tante*. Have you seen La Fonda? I've been up to the attic twice, and there's nobody home."

"Have you lost your mind?" She noted that he had a hard time standing.

"I miss her. I can't eat. I can't sleep. I can't pray." He swayed almost falling down.

"You know where she went! What's happened to you? Your hair is matted and you look dirty. Did you lose your job at the *boucherie?*"

"Appears I did."

"You're a mess." Camelia gave her nephew a disgusted look.

"I need to see her, *Tante.*"

"The last thing she needs is agitation, seeing you like this." Camelia saw that the little girls, licking their ice cream cones, were at the corner. "Andre, those little girls who live in my building, who're coming up the street, shouldn't see you drunk like this. They'll tell their parents that Andre Delacroix, who used to be a priest, was staggering drunk. What a scandal that would be. You're a disgrace to the collar."

"Where are Geetie and Gossie? They're not in an orphanage, are they?" he asked in a sobbing voice.

"For heaven's sakes, no. Do you honestly think your *Tante* Camelia would let her kin go to an orphanage? I've been taking very good care of your children. They are at Lily's home today, because I have to get these drapes sewed to get money to feed your children. They're being well-fed and well-clothed, better than they ever had before, if I must say so myself."

He stretched his arm out to touch his aunt in thanksgiving and tumbled onto the banquette.

"Goodness gracious! You go home and take a cold bath. Get going! And drink a pot of black coffee. I've got work to do." She walked up the front stairs and turned as an afterthought. "And cleanse yourself. Whew!"

Chapter 12

"Good morning, Pastor. I've come to discuss my great-nephew, Gustavo. He is to start the first grade. The boy is seven years old already, a little behind but he is very bright. He will catch up, and in a year or two, he will be able to skip a grade, so that he will be with children his own age." Camelia stood straight and tall, looking down at the pastor seated at his desk.

He did not invite her to be seated. The old pastor's indignation stirred within him. He remembered Camelia from the time she had come to the rectory to chastise Father Andre Delacroixe for not taking care of his children. *How presumptuous of her to think she can walk in here and tell me her great-nephew will start school and then skip a grade. It's probably that same bold, black boy she sent to the rectory once to come upstairs to our living quarters to give Andre a letter.*

Without a flinch, he responded, "Madame, there is no room in the school. We are full."

She trained her eyes on him. "Must he not learn his catechism, Father? Are children like my great-nephew, children of the men who take Holy Orders, those we most ardently respect and admire, are their children doomed to hell, never to receive the sacraments?"

His disapproval crept into his spiteful voice. "I have no obligation to Andre's mistress's children, and no interest in them whatsoever."

"Oh, but you do, especially if my client, Messieur Serou, editor of *The Picayune* publishes an editorial regarding the rights of priest's children, namely Father Andre Delacroixe's children, to receive a catholic education and become catholics. Why, where else are they to learn their commandments and take their preparation to receive the Eucharist?"

He winced, his cool manner completely erased by her threat. "Madame, you stop at nothing. Do you not?"

Camelia's expression remained above reproach, and she stood her ground, with her head held high. "You know Pastor Bourjaily, the thing that I love best about being a dressmaker and a midwife is that I have so many loyal, devoted friends in this city. I have the cream of the crop for my clients—doctors, lawyers, merchants, and especially newspapermen. It's so lovely."

She smiled bitterly and firmed her voice. "They invite me to their homes for lovely dinners, and we have become so close over the years, you can't imagine. They indulge me in every way. The winemakers give me wine. The bakers give me cakes. And the editor at *The Picayune* is one of my best clients. My advertising ads are always gratis. As a matter of fact, I helped bring him into this world. I've sewn all of his shirts since he was a little boy.

"He's always asking me if I have any interesting news for his newspaper when his lovely wife invites me to their home for dinner. He'd be interested to know that Father Delacroixe's children were not allowed in Catholic School because Father Bourjaily says that the school is full, and a priest's children could not receive their catechism lessons. How could they possibly receive the sacraments without their catechism lessons? And I happen to know that Monsieur Serou gives donations to the building funds and for the children's books. He happened to mention the figure to me. It was quite generous."

Father Bourjaily secretly feared the loyalty Camelia's gregarious clientele had for her. He had learned from Andre that many of her clients were rich Creoles who wholly trusted her judgment. Many were administrators in the city, like her son-in-law, Dominique Patteaux, and had much influence over their constituents.

The old pastor didn't miss a beat to digest Camelia's words. His eyes blazed in anger, as they averted her. He waved his hand and said in a stern manner, "Go speak to the nuns. See if they have room." He dismissed her coolly.

Camelia had a smile on her lips and let it bloom full, showing her beautiful, white teeth. *"Au revoir,* Father."

When she left the pastor's office, she felt weak at the thought of disgracing her sister's family by exposing Andre's family's name in the newspaper and the fact that Andre had children. Her sister didn't know that Andre left St. Maurice's Parish. They'd never told her. Camelia felt she'd spared her sister heartache by not telling her. She could never disgrace her.

Camelia had lost her sense of propriety, but the feeling of urgency to get Gossie into Catholic School overrode any sense of decorum.

She walked next door to the schoolyard where she checked on Gossie. He was staring at the children, playing tag, screaming, and chasing one another. He thought it great fun to run and scream, as they did, and wished he could go to school to run and scream and have friends to play with. He thought the playground was the school for he had never seen the inside of a classroom.

She waved for the boy to come to her. "Gosssie, are you okay?" She could see by the smile on his face that he was happy

"Yes, *Tante*. I like the school."

"Good. Stay here while I register you for the first grade inside."

As she entered the building, she remembered that the principal's office was the first office to the right. The door was open. She peeked in. A tall nun walked into the office from an adjoining room. "Madame, may I help you?"

"*Bonjour,* Sister. I would like to enroll my great-nephew in the first grade. I am Madame Arceneaux."

"Madame Arceneaux, it is unusual to enroll a child in the first grade at this time of year. The children are in their second semester already, and he would be so behind with reading and arithmetic, he would not catch up."

"I know this is unusual, Sister, but these are special circumstances. His mother is quite ill in the tuberculosis sanitarium, and she was so busy working to support her three children, she had not the time to register him sooner."

"Has the child a father?"

"Of course, he has a father, but that does not help the mother at all. His father is Reverend Andre Delacroixe. As you know, he was transferred to St. Maurice's Parish."

Silence hung in the room like a loud bell, clanging, for a long minute. "I... uh, well, I uh must speak to Pastor Bourjaily about this, madame. This indeed is a special circumstance." The nun's face flushed scarlet red.

"I've already spoken to him about this special circumstance."

"Today?" The nun looked at Camelia as if she had seen a ghost hovering over her.

"Yes, just before I came here."

The nun's eyes opened wide. She looked so scared that Camelia felt sorry for her. "Did he approve the boy's registration?"

"Of course, the pastor approved the boy's registration. He's just an innocent boy, Sister. He is not going to influence anyone in a bad way. He has only known love from his mother and father. Are you going to turn an innocent child away from learning the commandments and learning to be a Catholic or would you doom an innocent child to hell?"

"Oh, nooo! I would never…"

"I didn't think so, Sister. You are here to save souls, not to condemn them to hell. Will you direct me to the first grade classroom? I would like to speak to my great-nephew's teacher and see the classroom I will take him to."

"This way, madame."

Camelia followed the tall nun, whose black veil trailed behind her, to the first grade classroom. The principal opened the door and beckoned the first grade teacher over.

"Yes?" she asked, as she walked out of the classroom.

The first grade teacher's face reminded Camelia of a cherub. Camelia surmised she was a teenaged girl.

"Madame Arceneaux here wants to enroll her great-nephew in the first grade," the principal announced.

The cherub-face turned to smile at Camelia. "Madame, it is so late for the first grade. The children are reading already and adding and subtracting. Does the boy read?"

"Not as yet, but he is very bright. If he had books to read, I'm sure he would catch up very fast. His cousins and I will tutor him. I'm sure with books and tutoring, he will be able to catch up to second grade by next September, where he should be. And then, his younger sister can start the first grade in September, and he will be able to help her."

"This is most unusual," the cherub-faced nun said. "I don't even have an extra desk for him."

The principal winked at the young teacher and pulled her aside. Camelia thought she heard a gasp from the young nun.

The first grade teacher returned to Camelia with eyes cast down as if feeling shame for Camelia's nephew. "I can have a desk brought in for your great-nephew, Madame Arceneaux. You may bring him in tomorrow. I will also have his catechism books ready. Children's Mass begins at eight a.m. Have him here by ten of eight, the latest."

"Thank you. Just one thing, Sister. The boy limps as his father, Father Andre Delacroixe, did. I do not want the children to make fun of the boy and make him feel like a cripple. This boy has only known love from his family, and I don't want his loving nature ruined. If I find that you or any child makes him feel that he's not as good as the rest of the children, you will know my wrath."

"Yes, Madame. *Bonjour.*"

When she left the building and walked to the schoolyard, she craned to find Gossie. She spotted him playfully chasing a boy. "Come, Gossie!"

His happy eyes flew to hers to see if he heard right, a smile on his lips.

She nodded toward him and understood his hesitation.

"Come on, child."

When he was sure she wanted him to come to her, he ran as fast as he could with his limp.

With happy relief in her voice, she said, "I have you registered for first grade. You're going to start in the school tomorrow."

"*Tante*, I can't wait to go to the school again."

"You're a good boy, Gossie." She felt pleased that he was anxious to start school.

Camelia ran up three flights to the attic flat to talk to Andre and knocked on the back door. "*Tante*. This is unusual. Is something wrong?"

"Not at all, Nephew. I feel so good about it, I had to come and tell you right away. I've registered Gossie in the first grade. He's starting school tomorrow."

"That's wonderful. My boy starting school. Can you imagine? Did you have to talk to Bourjaily?"

"Yes, I did, but never mind that. Your *tante* took care of him. There's more I want to talk to you about. You seem better than the last time I talked to you. Are you still drinking?"

"Well, I have my moments when I'm lonely in the evening. I can't help it, *Tante*. I'm in hell without her."

"You don't have to tell me what loneliness is, Andre.

I've decided that you should go to her. I'm sure she is as lonely for you as you are for her."

"How do I go to her? She is in a sanitarium for the contagious."

"Get a room near the sanitarium. Find a job. Then, you can visit her every day."

"I don't know what kind of job I'd get."

"Don't act dumb, Andre. You've had all kinds of experience this past year. Go to the smithy. Go to the butcher. You've always been the bright one in the family, giving everyone else advice."

Andre knew what his aunt said was true. He was the sort of person who would gladly give advice to people with their problems or guide them to church. He would counsel them, hear their confession, but not necessarily befriend them. Counseling young boys was his forte, but he did not offer them his time other than in a professional way.

"Even if I do what you say, will they let me see her?"

She thought for a moment. "Well, I'm not sure what their regulations are for visitation rights. But if you got a job in that darn sanitarium, you could visit her every day."

He sat mute.

"Damn you anyway, Andre! Get off your ass, pack a bag and go to her. You're no good around here."

"You're right about that. What about the children?"

"What about them? Who's taking care of them now? You? No. They're already living at my place, and they don't seem to be suffering. Gossie's as happy as a clam that he's finally going to school. When he gets his books and starts to learn to read, he can teach Geetie to read. We'll work with him, Collette and I."

"Oh, it would be so lovely to see her. Do you really think I can go?"

"Go!"

Chapter 13

When Andre walked down the corridor of the tuberculosis ward, he passed a covered gurney. "May you rest in peace. Go with God," he murmured.

He walked past the doors marked BLACK PEOPLE ONLY, an area that was actually an enclosed porch modified to house black people with tuberculosis. The beds were pushed together so snugly that one could not walk between them.

With a heavy heart, he tried not to look at the ailing patients but looked at the numbers above the white, iron beds. The faint smell of vomit permeated the air through the odor of disinfectant.

It was his good fortune to spot La Fonda at the end of the row next to the window where he might have room to stand. He scooted along at the foot of the beds until he reached her.

She lay quietly, eyes closed, with her head turned toward the sun shining on her light brown face. He stood for a moment and gazed at her. He had never seen her look so peaceful.

He called her quietly. "La Fonda. La Fonda."

She opened her eyes and looked up to him. "Is that you, Andre, or am I dreaming?"

"Yes, it's me. It's me, your husband come to see you."

"Oh, Andre, what a lovely surprise. This feels like I'm in a dream, and I'm walking on a cloud in heaven."

He bent to kiss her, his face next to hers. "Oh, Andre, don't kiss me. I'm contagious. They told me that. Not to kiss my children, lest I give them tuberculosis. I don't want to make you sick either."

He rubbed her arm and nestled his face in her hair and kissed it. "I don't think that I can not kiss you, *ma cherie*. I've dreamt of you every day since you left *me*."

"And I of you. I've missed you so. I ache for you inside of me. How are the children?" She sat up and looked at him, anxious to hear of her family.

"Gossie is starting school. Geetie will start school in September. Blossom is keeping *Tante* Camelia busy, running all over the flat, getting into everything, and chasing the cat."

"I miss them so much. I still hear Blossom calling me during the night. Mamma. Mamma. I wake up and she's not there, and then I remember where I am."

He held his face close to her hair, trying to smell the familiar lavender scent that was absent. *"Tante* Camelia sent you this." He handed her a small package. "Open it. I don't know what it is."

She opened it to find a bar of Camelia's hand made lavender soap. "She knows how much I love her soaps. And your aunt…"

"Yes?"

"She's so good to me. I love her." La Fonda's eyes clouded up.

"I love her, too."

"Other than lonely, how are you, Andre? How are things at the *boucherie?*

"I'm not working there any more."

"And why is that? Did you find something more to your liking?"

"In a way. I'm going to be working here."

"Where?"

"Here in the sanitarium. I saw a notice that they needed a janitor. I applied for the job, and I start tomorrow."

"You shouldn't have to do that kind of work. Oh, that's so beneath you." As she curled up on her side, and furrows crinkled her brow, she let out a raspy cough.

"Oh, *chere*, should I call the nurse?"

"No, Andre. She may make you leave and you just got here. Stay with me."

"I got this job just until I can get a teaching job. The best thing about it is, I'll be near you. I can see you every day." He saw the first smile on her face, and the lines in her forehead disappeared.

"That's good news, Andre." She started to strain to breathe.

"Lie down and rest, *chere*. I don't want to tire you. Just rest." He knelt, brushing the side of the bed, and put his arm around her thin body and rested his head next to hers. "I want you so, *ma cherie*. My bed is so lonely without you. I can't sleep and I can't pray I'm so lonesome for you, but just to feel the warmth of your body makes me feel whole again. I've been a broken man without you. I've even been guilty of the sin of drunkenness, a sin that I totally detest. When a man confessed the sin of drunkenness in his confession, I would feel repelled. Then, I became the man I repelled without you."

She reached out to touch him—to comfort him. "I know you couldn't help it, Andre. You were unhappy."

His light caramel-colored hand, touching her chocolate-colored body never ceased to remind her how fortunate she was to have a man like Andre love her. She loved that he was so close to her and realized she had missed his clean, spicy scent, even his well-kept fingernails.

"You always say the right words to make me feel better. As long as I can be close to you and see you, I will be okay. Aunt Camelia was right. Being near you makes me whole again."

"Oh, you don't know how happy I am that I will get to see you."

Her expression changed. She looked up to him with a solemn face. "I have to tell you something, Andre. I may never get well. If you get a better job, you must leave here and go. You will need to support our children. I don't want them to wind up in an orphanage or bouncing from family to family like I did in my young life."

"Oh, don't talk like that, *chere*." He turned his head from side to side. "You'll get well."

"Promise me you'll try to get a better job and take care of our children. Please, Andre."

"I don't want to think about that. I just want to be with you."

She raised her voice. "Promise, Andre!"

He heard agitation. "I'll always take care of our children. I promise." He reached for her hand and kissed it. *"Cherie, je t'adore."*

She wheezed and let out a cough. She put her hand to her mouth to catch the blood spurting out.

A nurse rushed in, scooting along at the foot of the beds as fast as she could to reach La Fonda. She placed a hand towel over her mouth. "La Fonda, you've overdone. I told you to rest." She looked up at Andre. "Sir, I'm going to ask you to leave. The patient must have complete bed rest."

"I understand." He looked lovingly at La Fonda. *"Chere,* I will see you tomorrow." He kissed the air in her direction.

Her coughing prevented her from throwing a kiss. She leaned back into her pillow with a sigh and a cough.

He watched her struggle to get comfortable, walking backwards and waving. He stopped to listen to each wheezing breath until he saw her fall into a light sleep.

Andre closed his eyes and began to pray. He walked out of the room that smelled of death.

Chapter 14

As she scrambled through the old trunk in La Fonda's attic flat searching for warm long johns for the children, Camelia spied the red satin pouch at the bottom. The amulet spoke words to her. It told her that La Fonda had never placed it in her bed. This irritated Camelia, and then she questioned it.

She remembered the night she gave La Fonda the amulet. *La Fonda had a very simple prayer request. She only wanted for her family to be healthy and happy and for her children to go to school and learn like she never had a chance to.*

She also wanted for Andre to get a good job. She didn't want to take the amulet, but I insisted and plunked it into her palm. I guess I can't blame her for not wanting to agitate her husband. I shouldn't be that hard on the poor girl. But then, she prayed for health for the family. And she had emphasized health. Mmmm. Strange. Did she know she was getting sick?

As she beheld the starkness of the white sheets in the gloomy enclosed porch made into a sanitarium,

Camelia gazed at La Fonda, sleeping. She had never seen such peacefulness in La Fonda's face. The painful years of struggling to take care of her family alone had taken a toll on La Fonda. Camelia prayed that this rest would heal her.

Camelia saw her husband, Claudio, coming toward her, as she prayed for La Fonda.

Oh, Claudio, be with me as I try to comfort this dear, sick child. She needs me more than ever now to make her feel loved, and I need you to support me.

"I'm with you always, my love. You know that. Let's wake this child up and try to bring her some happiness."

"Hello, *chere*. It's *Tante* Camelia here." She tapped La Fonda's shoulder gently.

She opened her eyes to Camelia's loving smile. "Oh, Miss Camelia. How nice of you to come see me." She half-whispered, half-choked her greeting, and coughed.

"I brought you some of my nice date nut pudding."

"Oh, you so good to me! I love your date nut pudding."

"How are you, *chere?* I've missed you."

"Oh, I've missed you something powerful. And the children. How are my babies?" La Fonda looked up at Camelia with urgency for a happy answer.

"They're fine. Gossie's in school and loves it. Geetie plays with Blossom and the cats all the time. She dresses them and gives them water. Those cats never got so much attention in all their days."

"I'm glad. I'm glad." La Fonda strained to lift herself to a sitting position.

"Here, let me help you." Camelia helped her up and lifted the pillow for La Fonda to rest on.

La Fonda's eyes brightened at the thought of Andre. "You know what? I get to see Andre just about every day now."

"That's very nice, La Fonda. Lookee here, what else I've brought you." She pulled out a package from her burlap bag wrapped in paper. "Open it."

"Oh, my favorite. Your hand made lavender soap. I'd kiss you, Miss Camelia, but I can't. I'm contagious. I can't even kiss my own children." Sadness covered her face again.

"There's marshmallow soap in there, too." Camelia pointed to the package.

"Oh, thank you. You're too good to me with all this embarrassment of riches."

"I've brought an old flannel night gown of yours you might need that I found in your trunk. And here's what else I found." She pulled the red satin pouch out of her burlap bag.

La Fonda stared unblinkingly at the red satin pouch with wrinkles forming in her forehead. Guilt showed in her face. "Oh, Miss Camelia."

"I know why you didn't keep it under your pillow, La Fonda. I understand my nephew's feelings about amulets, and he's influenced you, too. You don't believe in them."

"I'm so sorry," she apologized. "I'll put it under my pillow now, if you want me to."

"You can't just put this little pouch under your pillow and expect a miracle. You have to believe in it. You've got to believe and want to get well bad—

badder than anything you've ever wanted. Do you believe you will get well?"

"Oh, yes, Miss Camelia. I have to get well for Andre and my children. And my baby. Oh, I miss holding my baby. I don't even know if I'll ever be able to hold her real close again, lest I give her my bad sickness." La Fonda's voice cracked.

"Say that you believe. Say, I believe I will get well." Camelia spoke in a stern manner.

"I believe I will get well." La Fonda repeated the words.

"And you must truly believe with your whole heart and soul."

"Oh, I believe with my whole heart and soul that I will get well." La Fonda placed the amulet under her pillow and looked at Camelia for approval.

"I have another surprise for you, La Fonda."

"What other surprise could there be?"

"What's the thing you want right now more than anything in the world?"

"To see my babies. Oh, I miss them something fierce."

She leaned back and closed her eyes, picturing her children.

"Well, go to the window and see your babies."

Camelia helped La Fonda out of bed and supported her at the window. La Fonda spied her children with Andre, looking up to her. She waved with a deep grin, then laughed and cried at the same time as she watched her children, throwing kisses. With a laugh, she threw kisses back and tapped on the windowpane in excitement. She wanted the sight of her children and Andre to last forever. "Oh, they look so big. Look at Geetie. She's grown, it seems. And will you just look at Blossom Rose. Why, she's not even a baby any more. She's fittin' into Geetie's old dresses now. And Gossie. Oh, my dear sweet son, Gossie. Mommy loves you!"

A stab at her chest broke the beautiful moment in the window. She fell to the floor.

"Mon Dieu, let's get you back into bed, *chere."* Camelia lifted La Fonda's frail body, helping her to her bed.

A nurse appeared. "Madame Delacroixe, it appears you've overdone yourself today. I told you to please stay in bed."

"I just wanted to see my babies," La Fonda said.

The nurse turned to Camelia. "I'm afraid I'll have to ask you to leave, madame. The patient has over-taxed herself. Visiting hours are almost over anyway."

"Oh, does she have to leave already? Seems like she just came." La Fonda looked on the verge of tears.

"Oh, but I think it did the patient good to see her children through the window," Camelia said.

"Madame, please," the nurse said.

"I'll be going now, La Fonda. I'll be back to see you soon." She threw kisses to her. "You precious child, get well soon. And remember what I told you."

"Will you bring the children again?"

Camelia heard the plea in La Fonda's voice. "Of course, *chere. Au revoir.*

"Au revoir, Miss Camelia. Tell them their *mere* loves them. Kiss them for me."

Collette

Chapter 15

Camelia was pleasantly surprised to find Melba answer her front door. She always found Melba in solitude, sometimes in her bed in pain, sometimes in her rocking chair.

"Why, Melba! You look quite well today."

"Yes, come in, Camelia. I just brewed a nice pot of coffee."

Camelia noticed that Melba had difficulty walking but was able to hobble with a cane into the kitchen to get coffee for her. "I'm so happy that you're feeling better, *chere.*"

Melba returned with a coffee cup. "Here, *chere,* I put cream in it the way you like it." She handed Camelia a cup of coffee with a shaky hand.

"How nice. And those look lovely." She nodded to the pastries on the tray and leaned over to take one.

"Yes, Silas, my dear boy, brought them for me this morning and put them there." Melba pointed to a small table. "Enjoy."

"What's the occasion?" Camelia peered over her coffee cup.

"I really am feeling better since you've been taking care of me. I just want to enjoy myself with you."

"I'm delighted, Melba. Maybe you could read my cards today."

"I will, Camelia. But first tell me. I've wondered about this for years. When we left off as friends, you were still with Rufus, weren't you? Was I the reason you split up? What happened after I didn't see you any more?"

"Heavens, no! You weren't the reason. You know what a roving eye Rufus had. Well, he left us when Rosalia was four years, long after you. I didn't know if he fell dead somewhere or not. It was worse than a death because I didn't know what happened. Rosalia and I were alone for quite a few years. I thought Rufus must have died somewhere and was never gonna come back.

"Then, I was asked to sew at a plantation in Baton Rouge. I stayed there for a while sewing draperies for the house and clothes for their three children, then dresses for Madame Dubourg and clothes for Monsieur Dubourg. By the time I finished all the sewing for the house and family, which took many months, I didn't want to leave. My Rosalia loved the country. She adored their oldest daughter, Katia. They played all the time. And, of course, it didn't hurt that I met Claudio, their quadroon stableman. Why, I never met a gentler man than him in my whole life. He was a widower and showed an interest in me right on."

"Did he ask you to marry him, or was it your idea?"

"He asked me to marry him, and I was walkin' on air. We married on the plantation. Then, I had Collette and we were very happy. Collette was so young, two years, when her daddy died in a horse accident. She doesn't rightly remember Claudio, but I tell her about him all the time."

"I see that you've had your share of heartache, too."

Melba moved to the sway of her rocking chair. "Whatever happened to Rufus?"

"I returned to New Orleans with my girls after Claudio passed on, and Rufus turned up one day to ask for money. Well, you could have knocked me over with a feather. I found out years later, he had been living with a much younger woman and had a child with her."

"Was Claudio anything like Rufus?"

She swung her hand past her face. "Oh, no. Not at all," she whined.

"What did this man, Claudio, have? This man you seem still in love with and unable to let go?"

Camelia looked across the room at Melba with a smile. "My husband, Claudio, was a perfect gentleman. He never put his hands on my body until we took nuptials, and then when he did, it was absolute heaven. I thought I was living a heavenly existence, when I was with my Claudio in bed. He never grabbed at me like Rufus used to. He would talk to me in bed and ask me if I wanted him to make love to me. When a man asks you the way he did with affection, how could you ever refuse him? When a man pulls back, you just want to pull him inside of you, that's what."

Melba's eyes crinkled around her shiny dark skin. "Oh, Camelia, you haven't changed a bit." A cackle broke from her mouth.

"Yes, I have changed, Melba. I don't go a day without wanting that man I love so much I could burst. I talk to him all the time and ask his advice."

"And does he give it to you?"

"Yes, he's the only one that tells me what to do in time of crisis, like when I'm birthing a baby. He always helps me when I need him."

"I see. Perhaps, some day you will not feel you need him as much as you do now. I know about your daughter, Rosalia. I've read her fate in the cards. But what of your other daughter?"

"My baby daughter, Collette, is married about a year and a half now. She has been trying to have a child. I don't know what's holding that up. I pray every morning at my altar for grandchildren before I die. Can you read her cards?"

"Yes. Bring the cards from the mantle in my boudoir and put them on this tea table. We'll see about Collette."

Melba's deft fingers shuffled the cards to mix them.

"You want to know about a grandchild?" she asked.

"Oh, yes. I'm quite anxious to know."

Her hands smacked three cards on the tea table. "I see your daughter is quite a self-determined woman with a mind of her own."

"Yes, my Collette doesn't let anyone fool her." Camelia looked pleased with Melba's observation.

"She's very much in love. I see passion in her life. Yes, she's quite a passionate soul."

"That's wonderful to hear, Melba. I love that my daughter has passion in her life."

She slapped a card down hard. "Mmm. Queen of Swords. A spiteful woman will do her harm."

"I wonder who that could be." Camelia stopped to think, pointing a finger in her cheek.

Melba suddenly tried to hide the burn in her stomach. Her quick heartbeat felt like a hammer banging against her chest, as she spotted the Death Card. She turned her eyes away from Camelia and looked down at the card, trying to hide her horror. She kicked the leg of the tea table hard. The cards tumbled to the floor. "Oh, my goodness. I accidently knocked my cane against the table."

"Oh, and just when it was getting interesting," Camelia said with a laugh. "I'll pick them up."

"No! Camelia, leave the cards. Silas will pick them up. I have a terrible pain in my back. I can't sit another minute. Will you make me a poultice, *chere*? I'd be forever grateful. I have to go and lie down."

"Of course. Why didn't you say something sooner about your back pain?"

"It's just when I sit too long in one chair. Oh, my back! It's killing me." Melba's heart pounded fast, as she thought of death in Camelia's family. She didn't know how to make the death scene in her mind go away. Her head started to throb with pain. *I wish I could stop it. How can I tell my best friend that she will have more misery in her life?*

Chapter 16

As Collette rode past the St. Louis Hotel in a carriage after visiting a friend on the edge of the *Vieux Carre,* she saw her husband, Dominique, enter the hotel. "Driver, please stop!" she called out through the window.

As the carriage stopped, a black praline lady blocked Collette's view of her husband. She turned to face Collette. "Pralines, Madame?"

Collette's eyes searched for a glimpse of Dominique, but his quick gate had led him through the opulent doors of the hotel.

"Madame, only ten cents for a box," the praline lady said softly. She stretched her arms out to offer a box of pralines.

Collette stared at the hotel entrance as guests entered, then turned her attention to the serious eyes that held her and would not leave. "Oh, yes. Very well. I'll take one box." Through a slit in her skirt, she reached into the pocket tied around her waist under her skirt and pulled out a dime. The praline lady smiled back at her, as Collette plunked the coin in her palm and took the pralines. *"Merci.* Driver, please drive past the French Market."

The praline lady waved, as the carriage drove away. *"Au revoir."*

Taking the longer way home gave Collette a few moments to reflect on what business her husband might have in such an establishment well after the lunch hour. She didn't think his position as a city administrator required him to go to the hotel, as she eyed the chickens hanging by their feet and the freshly caught fish wiggling in the diamonds of ice, as she rode past the French Market.

That evening, she stood at her stove and stirred the shrimp etouffe. Dominique surprised her with a squeeze at the sides of her breasts and a kiss behind her ear.

"Cher, I did not hear you come in." She turned to kiss him.

"And how is my beautiful wife and baby?" He rubbed her eight-month pregnant belly with reverence.

"We're fine, Dominique. How was your day?"

"It was good, but the best part of my day is coming home to you, *ma cherie."*

"Did you do anything unusual today, *cher?"* She looked up to his eyes, as they looked past her.

"No, my sweet. Nothing unusual."

As she brought food to the dining room table, she heard a knock at the door. "I'll get it."

Upon opening her parlor door, an octoroon woman, dressed in mauve taffeta, announced herself. "I am Madame Patteaux. Please tell Monsieur Patteaux, his wife is here."

"Who is it, *ma chere?*" Dominique called out from the dining room, as he walked into the parlor.

"It is your wife, monsieur," Tess Patteaux blurted out, as she made her way into the parlor.

Dominique's face blanched and his mouth opened in surprise.

Tess rushed to him with open arms. "*Bonjour, mon cheri.* I am so sorry I missed you today. The concierge told me that you paid a call on me. It has been too long."

Collette stood frozen unable to speak.

Tess grinned in Collette's direction, as she turned her head toward her, and then focused her shining eyes on Dominique. "Will you give us some privacy, *chere?* Leave us. We have much catching up to do."

Dominique turned to his wife. "You don't have to leave, *ma chere.*"

"Oh, it's fine." Collette rushed to her bedroom in tears. She sat on her bed and hugged her shoulders, rocking back and forth. Her worst fear was happening in her very own home. *Can this be true? Has he been seeing her at the St. Louis Hotel? Does he still love her, and she loves him? Does he make love to her now that I'm unattractive to him?*

Tess's words rang in her ears, and she couldn't listen to her piercing voice for another minute. *I have to get away from here, knowing that my husband is in my home with that woman who wants him and maybe he wants her, too.*

She looks desperate to have him for herself. Will he fall for her again? He did once. Oh, I can't stand it. I have to go— anywhere, just to not hear that woman's voice seducing my husband.

She grabbed a cape from her armoire and left the flat by the kitchen door with a broken heart.

Chapter 17

Tess's eyebrows danced in rhythm with her wild-cat eyes, as she strutted around the parlor.

Her cheeks quivered when she looked up at the lovely draperies and tapestries that Collette's mother had hemmed. She wore no diamonds to wink back at him. Thin silver threads, hardly noticeable, hung from her earlobes in place of the diamond earrings he had given her.

She had a hungry look about her. Her sharp cat's eyes roamed the furniture. "You're doing quite well, I see, *mon mari.*"

He ignored her reference. "What brings you here, Tess?"

"I hear you're living with a *metisse.* Did you marry your mistress because of her condition, poor thing? Tsk. Tsk."

"No, Tess. We tried for a year to have a child. She gave me the most glorious year of my life."

"No doubt." She arched her eyebrows and nodded. "You were always good with that." She laughed, and shot a look below his waist, pointing with her head.

He was not amused. "She is my wife, Tess, and I love her."

"Oh, Dominique. Tsk. Tsk. What is love? A feeling you have in your pepino for this young Negro girl when you're in bed with her and feeling her naked body?"

"No. It is a feeling we have for one another all the time."

"Hah! And you didn't have that same feeling for me when you felt my breasts and rubbed my nipples hard until I screamed for you to make love to me? You loved it when I screamed for you, didn't you, Dom? You told me you did, or were you lying to me?"

He looked away from her. He wanted to forget those passionate nights with her, but now she was here reminding him of the years they spent lovemaking. She brought back the memory of what a hellcat she could be in bed when it suited her. At other times, she bargained for sex, trading sex favors for clothes and jewelry, sometimes even money. *What does she want now? Surely, not me. She had me once and spat me out like a bitter seed.*

As he walked to the parlor windows, he looked down to see Collette, waiting for a carriage. Then, as a carriage stopped in front of his building and let some passengers out, Collette negotiated a ride, most likely to *Faubourg Marigny*, where her mother lived.

"Tell me, Dominique. were you lying to me when you professed your love for me and asked me to lie naked with you night after night?"

"No, I was not lying to you."

"Then, are you lying to that poor negro girl who just left in tears?"

"No. I am not lying to her. And she is not a negro. She is a beautiful quadroon."

"Oh, a koowadrooon. A koowadrooon. That's a word for black, I believe. You can't be truthful to both of us now, can you? Tell me, which marriage was a fake? Ours or the one with the *metisse?*"

"Stop calling my wife despicable names!"

She laughed at him in mockery and pasted a phony smile across her face, showing her large teeth.

He turned from her mischievous laugh. "Neither marriage was a fake. You wanted your freedom to *passe de blanc.* I gave you what you wanted. A divorce. Everything in our home and money. Now, Collette and I are married."

"You can easily remedy that. I expect she'll come back for her few belongings, and I can move in within the week. We can have those same passionate nights we had before." She looked up at him for approval, her white teeth glistening through her pressed smile.

He rebuffed her claim in a serene manner. "I am married to this beautiful woman. Collette's and my marriage was blessed in the church in the eyes of God as yours and mine never was. You had your reasons for not taking nuptials in the Catholic Church—in case you wanted to leave me. I understood that. We are divorced, Tess. That means you have no right to move into our blessed home."

"We were never divorced, my pet." She spoke through a forced smile.

"Yes, we were."

"Nay. I never drew up the papers." She whispered in ridicule.

"But I did, madame."

Her doubting eyes snapped back at him. "Nay," she hissed softer, knowing she had lost the bargaining tool she had come with.

"I did not know where to have the divorce document sent. You would not tell me what city you were moving to."

"I recall no such thing," she spat back at him.

"Let me refresh your memory, madame. You did not want me to accompany you and your family to wherever you were moving to, so I would not give your little secret away. Remember now?" He raised his eyebrows and pointed his head towards her. "You were passing or did that not fare so well? Did someone suspect your black blood?"

Her quicksilver mood changed to dismay. She looked down, trying to think of her next move.

"I will have my lawyer deliver the divorce document. Do you have a card with your address, madame, or are you in transition?"

Her mouth dropped her pressed smile. "I am staying at the St. Louis Hotel. Here is my card. You may call on me at my hotel when you want to talk sensibly."

"Tess, please don't call on us again. My wife is in a delicate condition. Please do nothing to upset her. If you will excuse me, I must go to her."

"Dominique, Dominique. You were always the soft one. Weren't you? Go to her? Where has she to go, my pet?" She placed her fan behind her head and gave him a wicked eye. Then, she extended her little finger beyond the fan.

Her pathetic overtures disgusted him. He avoided eye contact with her.

As she advanced toward him, she pulled her decolletage lower enabling her breasts to bounce as she walked. She tied her arms around his neck and pressed her breasts against him. Her warm lips tried to reach his. She leaned her cheek toward him and waited for a kiss. When he turned his head from her, her cheeks bloomed red and her eyes flushed hot.

Her eyes looked up to him in a devilish dance, as she slumped her body closer to his. He backed away in trepidation. "Oh, Dominique, *cheri*, why are you doing this to me? Don't I mean anything to you? All those beautiful years we had together. We can have them again, my beautiful husband. I will do anything for you."

Dominique caught the desperate need in her voice. He knew she would never have come to him if she had been faring well financially. Her need to put Collette down showed her desperation for his support. It sickened him the way she shamelessly threw herself at him. *How many other men has she made a play for before me? I'm probably her last resort. She has no love for me nor I for her.* "I am not your husband. Madame, please! I must go to my wife!" He extended his arm towards the door.

Briskly fanning herself, she sashayed to the door, her taffeta skirts swooshing past him. He merely nodded, as she passed him.

"Dom, I know that you haven't had time to think about what you really want. It all happened today. But maybe tomorrow, you will want me, and I will be ready for you as I have always been. I love you, Dom. Oh, why do you think I came back? I could not live without you!" She feigned a sob. *"Au revoir, cheri."*

He heard her heels bounce against the wooden stairs, as she descended. With each bounce, his heart flipped. He held in breath and waited for her to be gone, so he could go to his pregnant wife in private and plead forgiveness for such an intrusion.

Chapter 18

"Mamma, please open up. Mamma, Mamma!" Collette screamed, as she banged on her mother's front door. She'd held back tears in the carriage, but by this time, she could not hold back her heartbreak.

Camelia opened the door to a hysterical daughter. "My land, Collette, what is the matter?" She held her arms out and embraced her. "Come in, *chere.*"

"Mamma, he loves her!"

"Who?"

"Dom. He loves the woman he was married to."

"Oh, I'm sure you're mistaken. He loves you. I'm sure of it. Please, sit down and let me take your cape."

Collette cried uncontrollably. "How can this be happening to me? I'm finally going to have his baby, and he's in love with her."

"How do you know this?"

"She came to our flat and walked in as if she owned my home and talked to him like he is still her husband. She asked me to leave them alone so that they could have some privacy."

"And you did as she said?"

"Yes." Collette nodded.

"Why did you leave them?"

"I was in such a state of shock, I couldn't stay in that flat another minute."

"You shouldn't have left them alone, *chere*. Not that anything will happen, mind you, but you shouldn't have left. She sounds like a barracuda, coming to your home and acting like that. I'll make you a cup of chamomile tea to calm you."

Collette rose to follow her mother into the kitchen.

"Oh, *Mon Dieu!* Oh, Mamma!" She leaned forward and grabbed the arm of the settee.

"What is it?" Camelia rushed back into the parlor.

"I have pain, Mamma. Pain!"

"Oh, Dear Lord in heaven, come into my bedroom and lie down. You've been too upset."

"Oh, Mamma. Do you think the baby's coming?"

"It's much too soon, *chere.*"

"What else could this horrible… Oh,…" Collette bent over in pain.

Camelia helped Collette to her bedroom. "Let's take these uncomfortable clothes off. I'll slip a flannel gown on you." She ran to her armoire and pulled out a nightgown. She unbuttoned Collette's dress. "Lift your arms up, darlin'."

"Oh, not now, Mamma. I can't." She strained against the bedpost and let out a cry.

Camelia waited a moment in fear. The pains were coming fast. She pulled Collette's dress off swiftly, slipped a nightgown over her head, and pulled off her shoes. "Get into bed, *chere*. You'll be more comfortable."

"Mamma, why is this happening to me? What does this mean?"

"It means you have been too upset. It may be false labor. We don't know yet. Just try to lean back against the pillows and relax. Just rest, *chere*. Say a prayer. I'll go and put the kettle on for chamomile and raspberry leaf tea. Pray, Daughter."

Camelia went to the kitchen to prepare tea and get her little black bag ready in case she had to deliver her grandchild that night. Her hands shook, as she checked her bag and poured boiling water over the tealeaves. She had delivered hundreds over the years but had never been this nervous to deliver a baby.

She hurried back to Collette and set the teacup on her writing table. "How bad are the pains, Daughter?"

"Bad, Mamma. Bad." Collette shifted her body from side to side and cried in piercing pain.

Camelia pulled one sleeve up, felt Collette's cool arm, and pulled the duvet over her. "Now, I'm just going to ask you to take a sip of this tea, *chere.*"

"Oh, Mamma. I don't think I can sit up."

Camelia reached behind Collette's back and gently pushed her up. "I'll help you sit up, my sweet. Now take a little sip. It will help you."

Collette took a tiny sip and lay down.

"Oh, Mamma. Pain! Pain!"

"I know, my precious one. I know."

Collette writhed in pain, her arms flailing. "I feel wet, Mamma. It's all wet in bed. What is this?"

"Oh, your water bag broke. It means this is the real thing, and you're going to have a baby tonight."

"I didn't know it was going to be this hard to have a baby. Oh, Mamma!"

Camelia checked to see how far Collette was dilated. Her hands trembled when she realized Collette was close to giving birth. "You're coming along fast, *chere*. Many women go for hours and hours of labor pains before they get to this stage. I'll get a dry nightgown and some dry sheets."

"No, don't leave me, Mamma. I don't care any more about a dry nightgown and dry sheets. I need you, Mamma. This is the worst day of my life. My husband is in love with another woman and I'm dying." Collette coiled from side to side and moaned.

"Oh, my dear sweet daughter, you're not dying. You're just going to have a little one."

"But I want to die. Don't you understand, Mamma? I want to die! Oh, God in heaven, take me!"

Camelia looked back in horror. Her daughter got out of bed and grabbed the bedpost. A pool of blood gushed beneath her, as she shrieked in pain.

"Oh, Mamma. I can't stand it. I can't stand the pain.

Give me something, Mamma. Can't you give me something?"

"Please get back into bed, so that your little one doesn't fall on the floor."

"It feels better for me this way." She continued to reach for the bedpost and lean on it.

"I know but…Oh, *Mon Dieu*, let me help you back into bed."

Collette got into bed and let out a curdled scream.

"Will you take a sip of this, chere?"

Collette writhed, turning her body form side to side. She pushed the teacup away from her, spilling the tea on the bed. "I don't want to drink. Pain! Pain!" she shrieked.

Camelia checked between Collette's legs to find she was further dilated.

"Oh, Mamma, do something for me. I can't stand it."

"Just try to breathe calmly, *chere*. Blow little puffs out of your mouth. Try it."

Collette blew small breaths. It seemed to calm her momentarily.

Camelia knelt next to the bed and held her hand, breathing with her. "You're going to have a baby soon. Just think pleasant thoughts of your dear, sweet baby."

A piercing pain jolted Collette. "Oh, *Mon Dieu!* What pain!"

Camelia checked under the sheet to find that Collette was completely dilated. "Grab onto my hands, my sweet, hold on hard and push with all your might."

"I can't push. Pain…"

"Push hard. Push. Push."

"I can't. I…"

"You can do this, Collette. Push as hard as you can. We want to have a baby. Don't we?"

Collette strained to push hard and whimpered.

"Thatta-girl. You're doing great."

The baby started crowning, as Collette screamed in pain. As the infant came through the birth canal, Camelia grabbed her in the bloody mess and cut the rubbery cord. Wiping the blood from the baby's mouth and nose, she saw that the infant was blue. With a broken heart, she whisked the baby away to her writing table.

"What is it, Mamma? A girl or a boy?"

She could scarcely get the words out. "It's a girl."

"Can I see her, Mamma?"

"Oh, you need your rest now, Collette. Just rest. I have to clean her off. She's quite bloody." She sucked the mucus out of the baby's mouth and spit it on the towel. Waiting for a sound, she held her upside down and tapped her fragile back with a finger to facilitate a breath. Setting her down, she rubbed the baby's back, massaging it, holding back tears. With trembling hands, she pushed on the baby's chest over and over again trying to get a breath. Refusing to give up, she rubbed the lifeless baby's back until she realized it was futile.

"What's the matter, Mamma? Is something wrong with the baby?"

"Oh, Collette!" She rushed to her daughter. "I don't know how to tell you this. Oh, God in heaven, why? why? These things sometimes happen."

"Is my baby?"

"Ma chere, this is the hardest thing I've ever had to tell you."

"Oh, no. Mamma! I can see it in your eyes and your trembling lips. Oh, no. My baby is not alive, is she?"

Camelia embraced her daughter, and they wept in each other's arms.

Chapter 19

"Oh, yes, Dom, it is you. Come, come. I am at my wit's end." Camelia put her hands to her head, then looked at her bloody hands and wiped them in her apron.

"*Belle-mere*, you look distressed. Where is Collette?"

"Dom, I have the worst news in the world." Camelia broke down in sobs.

"I have never seen you this way. Please tell me. Has something happened to Collette?"

"She has lost the baby. She went through a horrible fast labor, the fastest I have ever seen, and your dear child was born dead. I must go to her now. My suffering daughter is hemorrhaging something awful. I am trying to stop it and keep her alive." Camelia ran from the front hallway to her bedroom.

Dominique followed and stood in the doorway of Camelia's bedroom. Camelia felt her daughter's forehead and lifted her to a sitting position. "Drink this, child. Drink." Collette sipped the herbal tea and lay back down.

Camelia looked up to see a frightened stare in Dominique's eyes, looking across the room at her. "I don't think you should come in here just yet. This blood bath needs to be cleaned up, but I just haven't had time with more important things to do."

"I understand. Is there anything?" He stopped cold when he saw the dead infant wrapped in a towel lying on Camelia's writing table.

"Yes, there is something you could do. Go as quickly as you can to Dago Annie at 1185 Governor Nicholl. Tell her that Camelia Arceneaux can't stop the hemorrhaging for her daughter."

"Is that Dom who is here?" Collette raised her head from her pillow.

"Yes, Daughter. But not now. Just rest until we get the hemorrhaging down. Go, Dom. I can't leave Collette now. I must stay with her." Camelia checked the blood flow under the blanket. The pool of red flowed onto the bed.

"Yes, it's me, my love." He took two steps into the room, saw the blood bath on the bed, and backed up.

"You must go now, Dom. Tell her the yarrow and the shepherd's purse are not working. Tell her I am afraid for my daughter's life. Try to find a carriage quick. Go! Please!"

"My sweet daughter, you must keep drinking this, or I don't know what I'll do. You mean more to me than life."

Collette sat up with Camelia's help and sipped the herbal tea. She lay back down and saw a figure. "Is that my sister, Mamma?"

"Yes, it's Rosalia, *chere.*"

Horrified by the sight of the dead baby and the blood on her mother's hands, Rosalia held in breath. "Oh, my dear Collette, I was not here for you."

"You were the lucky one not to witness this death scene. I have lost my baby, Rosalia."

"Oh, Sister, I am so sorry." She walked across the room and bent to take her sister's hand. She knelt and stifled a cry.

"It's okay to cry, Rosalia. Mamma and I have been crying, and we're not crybabies."

"Oh, I wouldn't have gone to opera if I had known you were in labor. I could have helped."

"Give her this tea, Rosalia." Camelia handed Rosalia a cup.

Helping her sister to a sitting position, she beheld the sadness in her grief-stricken eyes. She held the cup to her sister's lips. This was the sister who she secretly envied for her beauty and her light quadroon skin compared to her own darker skin. They were from different fathers. Collette's father was a quadroon gentleman who worked on a plantation with the horses, and Rosalia's father was a black street entertainer who had deserted Rosalia and Camelia when Rosalia was four years old. Now, for the first time, her baby sister looked worn and older with deep sorrow in her eyes.

"Sip more, Sister. We have to get you well."

"I just want to rest. Will you stay with me for a little while?" Collette closed her eyes and tried to think of happier times.

"Of course."

"Did you know my father well, Rosalia?"

Yes, I did. He was a fine man."

"I can't really remember him. I was two years when he died in that horse accident."

"Yes. I was twelve. He treated me like his little girl. He used to give me pony rides and sing to me. He was better to me than my real daddy. Mamma was the happiest I ever remember her when she was married to your daddy, Claudio."

"Oh, I'm glad mamma knew real love. She loved him, didn't she?"

"Why, of course, she loved him. She talks about him all the time. You know that."

Camelia rushed into the room to check on Collette. "Please sit in that chair next to the writing table, Rosalia." She saw the blood still raging from Collette. *"Mon Dieu!* I pray that Dago Annie will get here soon. She is the best at this. Let's say a prayer until she gets here. Pray, Daughters, pray!"

Camelia and her daughters prayed together in unison.

Dago Annie marched into Camelia's boudoir with her black suitcase. "Everybody out of the room!" She eyed Rosalia and turned to Dominique. "And that means you, too. We don't need any man fainting in here."

Rosalia and Camelia walked toward the doorway and joined Dominique, looking back at his wife.

"You stay, Camelia. I might just need you. The rest—out!" Annie placed her suitcase down and took her long, black coat off and threw it on the floor away from the bed. "How long has this been going on?" Annie turned to Camelia with squinting eyes.

"Since the baby was born. Almost an hour."

"And the yarrow and shepherd's purse did not work, you say?"

"Yes. They did not work."

"The afterbirth hasn't come, has it?"

Camelia pursed her lips. "No."

"I'll take care of that." She scrambled in her black bag and took out an envelope. "You make a cup of tea with a teaspoon of these herbs. That'll take care of her afterbirth pains."

Annie checked Collette to note the flow. "I will massage here, *chere,* but pay me no mind. Close your eyes and relax. I must do this. It is most necessary, or I wouldn't."

"My baby. I haven't seen my baby. Will I see her?" She tried to turn her weak body.

"Your mother will bring her to you later, child. First, we must do this. Please lie still." Annie massaged Collette's abdomen, pushing downwards and backwards into her pelvis.

"Ow! It hurts, Annie."

"I know, but I must do this."

"It's tender. Oh, pain!"

"Yes. Please, don't squirm. The sooner I can do this, the sooner we will get through it." Annie continued pushing downwards and backwards amid Collette's screams. "I know it hurts. Just try to relax."

Camelia entered the room and looked solemnly at her daughter, writhing below the large, working hands of Annie.

"Set the cup down, Camelia. We must do this first to get the afterbirth out or else…"

"Can I help you, Annie?"

"Watch how I'm doing this. You may have to take over later if I need a break."

Camelia walked to the other side of the bed and watched Annie with close attention. She stroked Collette's hair and sang to her.

Annie continued pushing down into Collette's pelvis.

Camelia's hymn seemed to soothe Collette, and her body stopped moving. Annie felt hardness beneath her hands, and continued pushing down and backwards into the pelvis. As she pushed hard once again, the afterbirth appeared, and Annie pulled it out followed by a gush of blood and clots.

The two midwives watched the blood flow out of Collette with dread.

Camelia scarcely got the words out. "Annie, what should we do? I can't think straight. She's my world."

"Brace your daughter. Lift her arms and let her squeeze your hands and push on you with all her might." Annie took an eyedropper out of her bag and filled it with cayenne. She pushed the duvet to the foot of the bed, separated Collette's legs, and squirted the cayenne directly into her vagina.

A blood-curdling scream bounced against the walls, and Camelia, seeing the heart-wrenching pain in her daughter's face, also yelped like a hurt dog. "Push, Collette, push!" Camelia screamed. "Push me through that wall if you have to!"

"Thirteen, fourteen, fifteen, sixteen, seventeen, eighteen, nineteen, twenty drops. That should stop the damned bleeding." She waited a few moments, as she packed her bag, and then checked Collette once again to see that the bleeding had subsided. Relief washed over her face. She gave a happy nod to Camelia.

"Oh, I don't know how I can ever repay you." Camelia cried through her words. "You gave me my life back. What can I do for you?"

Annie reached down for her coat and put it on. "Well, for one thing, you can sew me a damned new coat. I've worn this moldy old coat here through more rain storms than I can remember, and it's got holes in it."

"Oh, I'll sew you the best coat money can buy, gratis, of course. I will, Annie. And I'll be indebted to you for life."

"No need for that. Just sew me a coat. I've got to get back to my little mother, waiting on me. She was in labor when Dominique came for me. She should be about fifteen minutes apart by now. I wanted to take care of your girl first."

"You don't know how I appreciate that."

"Now give your girl that tea you made for her afterbirth pains, and give it to her three times a day until her pains are gone. And Collette, *chere,* you'll be feeling better. I promise. I'll come and check on you later after I deliver a baby"

"Thank you, Annie. Thank you so much."

"Au revoir."

Camelia turned to see Rosalia in the doorway, as Annie was leaving.

"Is my sister all right, Mamma?" Rosalia pinned a worried look toward Collette.

"Yes, thank God. Collette has survived an unfortunate stillbirth. She will need plenty of care. Annie has done her thing. Rosalia, we must clean this bloody mess. I need a *blanchiseusse*. Go up to the attic and get—Oh, what am I thinking?" Camelia slapped her palm on her forehead. "La Fonda's not there. Oh, dear Lord, how I miss that girl."

Chapter 20

As Camelia lifted the duvet, she eyed pockets of blood splotched on the bed. "I'll just pick up these sheets from the floor. I'll probably need someone to help me lift you, so I can take the sheets off the bed."

"*Mere,* I can lift my sweetheart off the bed." Dominique swooped Collette up into his arms.

"Take her into the next bedroom," Camelia said.

He carried her to the bedroom that used to be hers. The air was fresher without the smell of death. As he lay her on the bed, he held his cheek to hers. "I am so sorry that we have lost our baby, and I'm sorry for the distress you have had last evening. I feel guilty for causing you such misery."

"I have lost my little girl and my husband in one night," she said.

"You have not lost me, *ma chere.*"

"The woman who came to our home seems to still lay claim on you. She acts as if she's still married to you and appears to still love you. Do you love her?"

"No, darling. I love you, only you. And as for her love for me, it is just a façade."

"Why did you not tell me that you went to the St. Louis hotel?"

"I didn't want to upset you."

"For what reason did you go to her?"

"My lawyer asked me to meet him there. He wanted to explain that she was back in town and wanted more money, and what would I agree to. Also, he wanted to deliver the divorce document personally in my presence so that she would not deny that she received it. He has had some underhanded experience like this in the past. The desk clerk told us that she was out. He must have told her that Monsieur Patteaux paid a call."

Collette moved her head away from him and closed her eyes. "I don't know what to think right now. I am so tired."

"You must believe me, *chere*. I did not know her address when she left me. She moved away with her parents to another city and did not want anyone to know their whereabouts. They were trying to *passe de blanc*. Why she returned, I do not know."

"Do you know what we had?" She turned her head to look at him with wistful eyes.

"I, uh, heard you say…"

"We had a little girl, Mary, but she was born dead."

"I am so sorry, ma Cherie."

"I had my little Mary, but I will never be able to hold her in my arms and love her the way I wanted to. Dom, I never got to hold my baby. Can I hold her?" Collette asked with pleading eyes.

"Can we see the baby, *Mere?*" Dominique called out.

Grief-stricken, Camelia came in with a mournful and tired face and carried the baby dressed in a white christening gown. The pain of the loss of her very own granddaughter pricked at her. She hid the gnawing feeling in her heart from her daughter. Muffling a sob, she handed the dead infant to Collette. "I baptized her Mary, as you requested," she said.

"Look, Dom, she has your light skin. She looks like you. She would have been a beautiful girl. Oh, my Mary. How beautiful you are. Why? Why, God? Why did God do this to us?" Harrowing tears escaped Collette's swollen eyes.

"I don't know if God did this to us, my darling wife.

Please forgive me if I have upset you or caused this."

"Oh, my baby, I wish I could breathe life into you," Collette said with a cracking voice.

Camelia looked back at the heartbreaking scene of a mother and father with their dead child and left the room for Collette and Dominique to mourn in privacy.

"I'm sorry, so sorry. I beg you to forgive the intrusion in our home, *ma cherie,*" he pleaded on his knees, as he reached out to caress the cold arm of the baby corpse. Their cries smothered all other sounds in the house.

Chapter 21

Collette ran to her telephone. "Hello."

"May I please speak to Monsieur Patteaux?"

"He is at work at this time of day. May I ask who's calling?"

"This is Madame Patteaux calling."

There was a moment of silence until Collette composed herself. "You were told not to contact us, were you not?"

"This is simply a courtesy call to thank him."

"Thank him?"

"Yes. Please thank him for me for his generosity. And tell him I most graciously appreciate him."

Collette was speechless.

"You will give me that courtesy and thank him for me, won't you?"

"I will tell my husband that you called, madame, even though I owe you no courtesy. Please do not call our home again." Collette's face burned hot. She remembered the last time she'd encountered this woman. It was the worst day of her life.

"Yes, who is it?" Camelia stared into the sorrowful eyes of a disheveled woman draped in black at her front door. The woman's face was pallid and her eyelids drooped.

"Madame Arceneaux?"

"Yes."

"Madame Melba Loutierre told me to see you. She is an old friend of yours?"

"Why yes. Come in." Camelia was happy to hear that her friend Melba had broken her solitude.

"Please, sit and make yourself comfortable." Camelia pointed to a chair and was anxious to know what this woman had to say. "Is Melba ailing?"

"No, she is better, thanks to you. She told me of your kindness and said if anyone can help me in my predicament, it is you." The woman sank into a soft, upholstered chair.

"How do you know Melba?"

"I've known her for years. I used to go to her regularly for the tarot reading. She is very good." The woman opened her eyes wide and cocked her head toward Camelia. As she moved her body forward, she choked in a spasm of coughs. She coughed more violently, shaking uncontrollably.

"Are you ill?" Camelia's knitted brow showed concern.

"Nothing a good meal wouldn't cure." The woman's eyes shifted toward the kitchen.

"Oh, sure. I've got some mutton in the oven and some eggplant. Come. Come. I'll make some hot tea for you to clear your throat." Camelia rose and gestured to follow her to the kitchen.

They followed the aroma of the mutton, and Camelia fixed a plate for her guest. "I'll brew some yarrow with fenugreek for your cough."

Camelia sat at the kitchen table and watched the woman ravenously devour the mutton and eggplant. She wiped the plate clean with her bread, sopping every trace of sauce in a circle. "You see. I have no means of support. That's my problem. I am alone."

"Where do you live?"

She cleared her throat and rubbed her lips together. "I have a room on Dauphine in the *Vieux Carre*. It's bad there." She scowled in a frightful manner. "People steal and pimp, you know. But what can I do?" She threw her arms up in despair.

"How did you live before?"

"I had family to take care of me, but my parents have passed on. And I had a husband, but he left me."

"Do you have no way to support yourself?"

"No, I don't. I do not come from a working class family. We come from money. Yes, we did." She looked up at Camelia for recognition. "There was always money for fine clothes and opera and good food. But all that is gone. Gone! I've sold my jewelry. Yes, my jewelry that *mere* gave to me. Can you imagine? Why, *mere* would turn over in her grave."

"Well, you'll just have to learn to support yourself before you wind up in the streets."

"I don't think I can do that. I have never been trained to make money. It was not in our family plan."

"You'll have to learn."

"Learn what?"

"I've supported myself and my two daughters by sewing. My second mother-in-law, Moses's mother, God rest her soul, taught me to sew clothes, embroider, and sew draperies. I worked my fingers to the bone when I came back to New Orleans after Moses passed on. Now, I have a wonderful clientele that supports me very well." Camelia's brainstorm hit a high pitch of excitement in her voice. "I could teach you!"

"What a harebrained idea that is. Me sewing. Hmmphh."

The woman gulped her herbal tea and shook her head.

Camelia's demeanor changed. "Listen here. Who is supposed to take care of you? Do you want to wind up in the District, spreading your legs to feed yourself? Huh? Huh?"

The woman straightened and shuddered. "No. I don't want to do that." She put her head in her hands. "*Mon Dieu.* I don't know what to do."

"Come into my dining room. I sew in there where the big windows give me plenty of light." The woman reluctantly left the toasty kitchen to follow Camelia.

"See this sewing machine." Camelia pointed to the sewing machine at the tall windows, the sun shining down on a yellow gown, flowing from the machine down to the floor. "It is my bread and butter. How else do you think I make money to live here and feed my family? I don't have a man. Yet we live quite well. My daughters wear beautiful clothes, because I sew them. If I didn't sew, God knows what kind of clothes we'd have to wear. I sew lovely gowns for my girls from the remnants from my customers. You could do the same."

The woman let out a huge breath. "You make it all sound so easy."

"Life isn't easy. The sooner you learn that, the better off you'll be. Sit down and hold this material here. Grab it! Hold it under the foot of the machine. Move it up. Move it up and pedal the machine. That foot pedal there." Camelia pointed down at the pedal. "See? It's not that hard if you pay attention."

She pedaled for a few seconds and gave up, throwing her hands up. "Oh, I don't know if I'm meant for this. And who in the world would I sew for? I don't know many people in the *faubourg* any more. I've been away for two years."

"Let's sit in the parlor, and I'll think of who you could sew for." Camelia stuck her finger in her cheek and thought of who asked for her services last that she didn't have time for. "Oh, I know!"

"Another harebrained idea?"

"The nuns! *Parfait!* They always have sewing to do and it's mostly straight sewing. You could sew a seam, can't you?" Camelia asked the woman with such exuberance as if they were best friends.

She looked at Camelia as if she were crazy.

"They mostly need their habits and veils sewed up in a straight seam. And with all the postulants coming in all the time, they don't have time to keep up. But, of course, they'll want you to sew for nothing." She stopped to think a moment. "You must have a price list to present to them. So much for a habit, so much for a veil, so much for bloomers." Camelia burst with enthusiasm from her idea.

"Bloomers?" The woman broke into a howl of laughter.

"You don't think nuns wear underwear?" Camelia joined her laughter. Then, in a serious tone, she said, "This must be a business. I know the tailor who sews for them when they can't get women to sew gratis. I will get his price list and you will price your items a bit lower than the tailor they use. They will always take you over him if your prices are lower."

"I don't think I can do this. I've never done domestic work," she moaned.

"Well, it's about time you learned," Camelia said.

"I don't know if I can do it. Oh, I don't know…"

"I can show you straight seams. Come tomorrow at eleven in the morning. I should have this opera gown finished by then. I am very busy, but I can give you an hour a day."

"Oh, but what if they ask for my services gratis? They will speak of their vow of poverty, and I will never be able to refuse them." The woman put her hands to her face in dismay.

Camelia stood over her with eyes open wide. "You tell them how hungry you are and how poor you are. They will even feed you."

"Feed me?" The woman appeared awed by Camelia's words.

"Of course. And tell them you need the money up front for food. They will feed you and pay you. The poor always help the poor."

"Oh, you are as kind as Melba said you are. I didn't want to come here. No, I really didn't." She waved her index finger back and forth. "But I'm happy that I did. Who else would help me but a woman like you? I've met some of your patrons. They had nothing but kind words of your benevolence."

Camelia softened at her compliments. "Where did you meet my patrons?"

"At the St. Louis Hotel where I was staying when I first returned to the city. I can see why Dom fell in love with your..."

Camelia's hands trembled, as she gasped in horror. "You are the ex-wife! Tess Patteaux!" She stared aghast at her with unveiled contempt and covered her mouth.

"I am Tess. Yes. And destitute. Does that make you happy?"

"No! I am not happy at any of this. Not for you. Not for my daughter or her husband. You left a good man like Dominique for this life? Why?"

"My fertile years with him were quite enjoyable, my happiest years. I must admit. But another world kept calling me—the white woman's world. And he, an octoroon, did not fit into that world."

Camelia could not conceal her resentment at Tess's racist remark. "You turn on your own and then you come to your own for help. Hmphh! You can't expect Dominique to take care of you for the rest of your life after you have left him and humiliated him by trying to *passé de blanc*."

Camelia looked down at eyes of despair. "No, I don't rejoice in other people's miseries. But you have caused my daughter so much sorrow. She lost her baby after you barged into her home, pretending you were still with her husband." Camelia pulled at her hair. "*Mon Dieu.* You don't know how much trouble you've caused my family. Oh, no." Pain stabbed at her heart. She felt squeezed between the love for her daughter and the desperation of this starving woman with no one to turn to but her.

Melba knew I could not turn a needy woman away. Not even this woman. She held her chest, trying to squelch the torn feeling in her heart. Yet, she could not turn Tess away.

Her mouth went dry. "I have a responsibility to my daughter, but that may be hard for you to grasp. You're not a mother. You can't understand how a mother feels toward her children. You must promise never to go to my daughter or her husband again. You must leave them alone!"

Camelia paced the parlor back and forth. She thought of the misery of Collette losing her baby, Mary. She heard the horses whinny outside and the clop-clop of the horses' hooves coming to an abrupt stop. She parted the lace curtains at her parlor windows to see her daughter, Collette, stepping down from a carriage.

"Oh, my daughter, Collette, is coming to visit. Please leave by the back door so that you do not confront her again. Oh, please don't cause her any more anguish," she said with urgency in her voice. "Oh, no! You can't leave by the back door. You must always leave by the same door you enter my home. I'll tell Collette to come in by the back door, and then you leave by the front door."

"Will you still help me tomorrow?" Tess Patteaux's haggard face held eyes with a look of despair.

"Yes, if you promise never to bother my daughter and her husband again."

"Hmphh. God knows I have bothered that man enough. He has no more money to give me."

"Promise," Camelia shouted.

"Yes. Yes. Yes. I promise."

Camelia ran out of her front door. "Collette, honey, how nice of you to visit. *Chere,* will you walk around to the kitchen door? There's a rotted step here with some others that are shaky. Silas hasn't gotten around to fixing them. I don't want your pretty foot to fall through."

"Yes, *mere.* I'll go 'round the back." Collette waved to her mother and threw a kiss.

Camelia ran back into the house and pinched her fingers in nervousness, as she gazed through her parlor windows. "She's going 'round the back way. Please leave! Hurry! And come 'round the back way tomorrow so you can leave by my kitchen."

"Bless you, Camelia Arceneaux." Tess bowed her head in Camelia's direction and walked unsteadily toward the front door. "You are the person your friend said you are."

Chapter 22

Collette stared at the ringing telephone, reluctant to answer it. *If it's that woman, Tess, again, I'll tell her to quit calling.* "Hello." She spoke louder than usual in an agitated tone.

"Hello, daughter," Camelia greeted.

"Hello, Mamma."

"Is anything wrong?"

"No, nothing wrong."

"*Chere,* could you do me a favor this afternoon?"

"What is it, Mamma?"

"I want to visit La Fonda at the hospital. She needs a few things I need to take to her. I'm getting a late start today, because I had to finish a dress for Madame Serou, the Picayune's editor's wife, my best patron. I couldn't disappoint her.

"I'd like to leave the children with Madame Le Doux until you can come by to get them, take them to my place, and watch them until I get back. I should be home before dinnertime. Could you do that for me?"

"Why, yes, Mamma. I'd be happy to watch the children. I'll leave shortly."

Collette took a carriage in the interest of time. When she arrived at Madame Le Doux's flat, the children ran to her in excitement. "*Tante* Collette! *Tante* Collette!"

"Did you come to play with us?" Geetie asked.

Collette picked Blossom up. "Yes, I've come to play with my little cherubs."

"The children are very happy to see you, Collette. And how are you feeling?" Madame Le Doux asked.

"I'm feeling well, thank you," Collette said.

"Your mother keeps so busy, teaching sewing every morning, and sewing for her patrons. I don't know how she does it. And she takes care of the little ones—at her age."

"Teaches sewing?" Collette wondered who her mother taught and how she found the time.

"Yes, the octoroon lady comes every morning for a lesson. Your mother is so kind to teach her to sew."

"Oh, I had not heard about the sew*ing lessons*. "Come, children, let's go across the hall to *Tante* Camelia's house. Madame Le Doux must have things to do." Collette turned to Madame Le Doux. "Thank you so much for keeping the children, madame. We appreciate your kindness. *Au revoir*."

As they entered Camelia's flat, Gossie ran to hide in Camelia's bedroom. "Find me. Find me, *Tante* Collette."

Geetie ran through the flat. "Find me too, *Tante* Collette."

Blossom giggled at the sight of her siblings running through the rooms. She pushed at Collette's chest to be let down. "*Tante*, find me."

"Okay, little one." Collette let the child down, and sat for a moment at the kitchen table. Blossom scurried about and was out of sight.

"I'm going to find you," Collette let out in a singsong voice. She heard scrambling and giggling. "Here I come, ready or not."

She walked through the dining room and parlor. "Where are you?" Collette exclaimed. She heard giggling, as she entered the front hallway leading to Camelia's bedroom.

In the bedroom, Collette ran to the alcove where Gossie's daybed was stored and pulled out at night. She peered under the small bed to find Geetie lying still.

"There you are," Collette sang.

Geetie screamed in delight. "Now, find Gossie."

"Oh, Gossie, where are you?" Collette tiptoed through the bedroom and looked under the four-poster, half-tester bed to find a few boxes and some dust bunnies. "Oh, Gossie," she sang. She opened the large armoire to find Gossie, hiding behind gowns and coats. "Oh, there you are, my little boy."

Gossie screamed in sheer joy. "Oh, *Tante* Collette, how did you know I was there?"

"I didn't know until I found you, my handsome boy."

"Now let's find Blossom," Gossie said.

The giggling children followed Collette, passing the parlor and into the dining room. She looked first under the dining room table before entering her old bedroom. Little Blossom lay quietly under her crib with her thumb in her mouth, holding her blanket.

"I found you," Collette sang.

Blossom giggled. "Find me again."

"I see my little girl is tired. Maybe she needs a nap," Collette said.

"No. No nap. I want to play."

"Okay, we'll play for a few more minutes, little one."

"Let's play animals," Gossie said.

They went into the parlor where Gossie proceeded to spring in big giant leaps. He looked down to his belly and put his hands into a pretend pocket.

"Are you a bunny rabbit?" Collette teased.

Gossie turned up his nose. "Naw, *Tante.*"

"A monkey?" Geetie asked.

"No, whatsa matter with you?" He leapt forward around the parlor and pushed at his imaginary, flapping ears, hopping in gigantic steps.

The children roared at his antics and Collette laughed until tears came to her eyes.

"Well, what am I?" Gossie stopped and gave them a look of disgust with his hand on his hip.

"Oh, I know," Collette said. "You're a kangaroo."

"You're a kangaroo, I know," Geetie said.

"Kangaroo," Blossom said.

"Oh, you knew, didn't you, *Tante?*"

"Me next," Geetie said. She proceeded to hop around the room and pointed toward her big ears.

"Aw, no. You can't be a kangaroo too," Gossie said.

"I'm no kangaroo," Geetie said. She hopped around the parlor and wrinkled up her nose and sniffed. She sniffed her brother's and her baby sister's arms from their shoulders to their fingers.

Gossie let out a loud belly laugh and Blossom imitated him in little giggles.

"Oh, I know," Collette said. "She's a little kitty cat, sniffing for her milk, and she has big ears," she teased.

"No! Not a little kitty cat," Geetie rebuffed and waved her hand at them.

"A big kitty cat?" Gossie said and laughed.

"No!"

"Oh, I know. You're a bunny rabbit hopping around and looking for carrots, aren't you?" Gossie said.

"You knew that all along, didn't you Gossie?" Geetie looked betrayed.

"It's just a fun game, Geetie. Don't get mad," Gossie said.

"Yes. You did very well for a bunny rabbit, Geetie." Collette looked down to see Blossom's eyes closing. She rose to put her in her crib. The children followed her.

As she covered Blossom with her blanket, Collette looked down at Gossie. "Who is the octoroon woman that *Tante* is teaching to sew?"

"Her name is like your name, *Tante*. Madame Patteaux."

Gossie innocently looked up at Collette.

Collette bit back a gasp and tried to remain calm. "Let's let Blossom sleep," she said with a broken voice.

She walked out of the bedroom trying to keep her composure, but she felt her heart tremble. "And *Tante* Camelia is teaching her to sew?"

"Yes, *Tante* Collette," Gossie said.

"What else do they do?"

"They eat. She is hungry when she comes," Geetie said.

"*Tante* Camelia always feeds her."

"I see," Collette said. "And do they talk like friends?"

"I guess so. Let's play marbles, *Tante*," Gossie said, and ran to the parlor.

❧

When Camelia came home, she found the children and Collette, playing marbles on the parlor floor. "Oh, you're playing. How nice."

Gossie looked up, grinning. "*Tante*, we have been playing all afternoon. *Tante* Collette shoots marbles very well."

"So, you had fun playing with *Tante* Collette?"

"Oh, yes. We played hide and seek and animals too," Gossie said.

"Blossom played too, but she's sleeping. And *tante* read us a story," Geetie said.

"How is La Fonda?" Collette asked.

The children's mood turned serious, as they looked up at Camelia.

"She's doing better. And your mamma said to kiss you for her," Camelia said.

The children ran up to Camelia for an embrace and a kiss.

"Children, will you play marbles while I talk to *tante* in the kitchen?" Collette said. Collette walked into the kitchen, waiting for her mother.

After Camelia entered the room, Collette let loose her feelings. "Mamma, how could you befriend her? I told you how she tried to seduce my husband, and you took her in like a friend."

"Who told you? Madame Le Doux?" Camelia's face turned serious with worry.

"She mentioned that you're teaching sewing, but the children told me who you're teaching. I could hardly believe my ears. Oh, Mamma. You've betrayed me." Collette cried hot tears.

"I did it for you, *chere.*"

"For me?!"

"Yes, the woman came to me, destitute and hungry, with no money. I thought I'd teach her to make her own way in life, so she wouldn't bother you any more."

"Why do you owe that woman anything?"

"I don't owe her anything. I just wanted to help her."

"You'd help the devil himself, wouldn't you? Did you forget the grief she has caused me? Apparently, you've forgotten what she cost me. My child! Mamma, I don't know if I could ever forgive you!" Collette left the flat with the slam of the door.

Camelia stood stunned, feeling her infidelity to her daughter for the first time.

Gossie and Geetie ran into the kitchen. "Did *tante* leave already?" Gossie's little face scrunched in disappointment.

"Yes." Camelia squeezed her eyes shut to hold in tears.

"She didn't even kiss us good-bye," Gossie said.

Chapter 23

Collette left her mother's flat in misery. The thought that her husband was giving gifts to his ex-wife was unbearable, and now her mother was feeding Tess on a daily basis and teaching her.

She hardly spoke to Dominique during dinner and retired early. She went to her boudoir to change into her nightclothes and reclined on the chaise longue.

Dominique entered the boudoir, undressed, and got into bed. "Come to bed, *chere.*"

"I want to sleep here tonight," she said.

He went to her side and knelt beside her. "What is bothering you? You've hardly spoken a word to me this evening."

"You know what's bothering me."

"No, I don't, *chere.*"

"You have not been honest with me." She turned her body away from him.

"In what way?"

"By not telling me that..."

"By not telling you what?" He held his arm around her.

"That you have been giving your ex-wife gifts," she said in a labored voice.

"That's preposterous!"

"Then why did she call our home and ask me to thank you for your generosity? Why?"

He heard the angered cry in her voice. "I have not been buying her gifts. And I've told her not to contact us again. Tess has a way of manipulating people. This is one of her tactics—to make you angry by fabricating a story."

Her eyes shuttered with discomfort, and she held back a sob. "I'm not so sure it's a story."

"Whatever do you mean?"

Her lips quivered. "Even my own mother has turned against me. She has befriended her and has her in her home every day."

"You must be mistaken."

She sat up and scowled at him. "I am not mistaken! Everyone helps this woman. My mother. My husband. And why? What hold does this woman have on you and my mother? Is she Jezebel herself? Don't try to talk me out of this. The children told me, and children do not lie."

"What did the children tell you?"

"The children have told me that *tante* has this woman over to her home every day and feeds her, and that her name is the same as mine—Madame Patteaux. And my mother did not deny it, when I confronted her. Oh, how could she do such a thing?" Collette could no longer hold back her emotions. She let out a shrill cry.

"There must be some explanation for this. I know one thing. Your mother would never do anything to hurt you."

"But you, my husband, the one who I make love to night after night. Do you want to get back with her, because she's octoroon? She is of a higher status, isn't she?" She could hardly get the words out, sobbing, looking at him with accusation in her eyes.

Dominique shook his head. "Oh, no, *ma chere*. She is out of your league. You are a much more elegant woman than she is in every way possible. Your beauty, your manner, your taste, your elegance, the way you talk, the way you dress, your modesty. It's all exquisite. You know that I have loved you from the moment I first laid eyes on you."

"I don't understand what's happening. First the loss of my child, then you, and now my mother, deceiving me. How much more can I take?"

"I only know that I love you, and I'm sure your mother loves you." He rubbed her back to soothe her.

"I can't believe either of you." She pushed his hand away.

'*Ma chere*, you know that I want you for the mother of my child, because I want my child to be just like you. I know you will be an exceptional mother. You know, I never pressed for children with Tess. I wasn't sure she would make the best mother. She was too absorbed with herself—not like you. You have always taken care of me just the way I love to be taken care of."

She turned to face him. "I wish I could believe you. I do."

"Please believe me, my sweet, and please don't stop loving me." He embraced her, and as he tried to kiss her with a hungry passion, she turned her head away from him. "I honestly don't know what I'd do if you stopped loving me."

He joined her on the chaise longue, and she cried in his arms. "Is this our first disagreement? We have done very well so far. Let's not stop our blessed marriage now."

"I don't know what to think any more. Do you give her gifts?" Her pained eyes looked up to his.

"No, my beautiful wife, I don't give her gifts. I only give gifts to you, and I shall do it more often."

She looked down with still-tear-filled eyes at the locket around her neck with his picture inside. "This was very special to me. I still remember the night you gave it to me."

"As do I. Remember what you promised me?" He gazed at her a long moment.

"Yes." She recalled the first time he'd made love to her.

"Tell me what you promised me that night."

Her wounded look did not leave her.

"Come on, my love. Tell me what you promised me. Remember?"

"I promised you that I would love only you," she said in a strained breath.

"And I have never broken my promise to love only you. Don't let her spoil this for us. Don't let her do it." He drew her closer to him and held her against his warm body. "I have not betrayed you, *ma cherie.*" The feel of her against his loins made him want her more than anything. "We will not start to sleep apart. That will never be."

He lifted her into his arms and took her to their marriage bed. Between the two pillows lay the red satin amulet. He smiled when he laid eyes on it. "And what does this satin amulet represent, my darling wife?"

"You know," she whispered.

"Yes, we prayed for a child. And we will pray for another one. I will have a glorious time putting my seed into you, my love."

She told herself he still loved her and wanted her, as she put her arms around him.

He cradled her close to him and kissed her with a long awaited hunger.

Chapter 24

My dearest Collette,

You don't know how it grieves me to think that I have caused you unhappiness. Believe me, Daughter, when I say that I never meant to hurt you. I realized after she told me who she was, and got over the shock of knowing, that she was not a friend of the family.

I made a decision to teach her to do something useful enough to earn a living, so she would not keep asking Dominique for more money. She finally confided to me that he gave her a generous settlement at the time of their departure. Then, when she came back to New Orleans, out of money and desperate, he agreed to pay her hotel bill through his lawyer.

In order for her to stop bleeding Dominique of his finances, I decided she had to have a means of survival. So, I taught her to sew and run a little business. She has started to get orders from the nuns, and I have introduced her to a tailor who will require her services.

I am praying that you and your husband will never hear from her again. She has promised me that she will not contact you.

What I did was for you my dear daughter, because I love you. Anything I can ever do to cause less distress in your life, I would gladly do for you. I would charm the devil himself to keep him away from you.

With pacific devotion,
Your loving mere

Collette was pinning up the last curl in her hair when she looked into the looking glass and saw Dominique's reflection, staring back at her.

"You look beautiful," he complimented.

Turning from her dressing table, she asked, "Dominique, how long have you been watching me?"

"Not long enough. Stand and let me see the gown your mother sewed for you."

She stood and twirled around to show the effect of the full sapphire blue gown. "Mamma outdid herself again, didn't she?"

His eyes blazed at the sight of her. "It's not the dress. It's your beauty that makes a beautiful feast for my eyes. I can't wait to have you on my arm and show you off."

"This is the first time I'll be going to opera since the ba…" She wiped a little moisture from her eyes with her handkerchief.

170   Dolores Else

"I know, my sweetheart. We'll have a wonderful night at the opera. And afterwards, we'll have dinner at your favorite restaurant, The Saffron. We'll eat oysters and crawfish and all of your favorites, and we'll sing. We'll sing our hearts out." He held her and whirled her around the room, singing.

"Dominique, you're in such a merry mood. What brought this on?"

"We're together, and you're feeling well enough to go out. Life is good."

As they left the boudoir, they heard a knock on their parlor door. Dominique answered it to find Camelia. "Why, *Mere*, what a surprise to see you this time of night."

"I just had to come tonight. Andre was over and is watching the children. I won't be staying. Collette, my dear, you look just beautiful."

"We're going to the opera, Mamma. The dress you had delivered to me turned out to be perfect. See."

Camelia lifted her eyebrows. "You look simply gorgeous in everything you put on. Dear Daughter, I couldn't go another night without your forgiveness. I can't sleep, thinking you won't forgive me. Did you get my letter?"

"Yes, Mamma. I understand now why you decided to teach her to sew."

Dominique chortled. "Only you, *Mere,* would be able to accomplish such a feat. Teach Tess to sew! Ha! I can't in my wildest dreams imagine it." He roared in a deep belly laugh.

Camelia brandished a hand at him, and turned to Collette. "Then, you forgive me?"

"Of course, Mamma. You know I couldn't stay angry with you." Collette embraced her mother.

"Oh, I feel so much better. You can't imagine."

"Would you like some hot coffee before you leave, Mamma?"

"Oh, no, I didn't intend to stay. The coachman is waiting. *Au revoir.*"

"*Au revoir*, Mamma. And be careful going down the stairs. Dominique, go with her. Help her."

Katia

Chapter 25

"Melba, my dear friend, how are you feeling today?"

"Much better, thanks to you." Melba waved Camelia into her parlor.

"I'm on my way to visit my dear friend, Katia. She's opened a dress shop. I've agreed to do the alterations. I just haven't had time to go there until today. My drapery business has been keeping me so busy." Camelia sat while she reflected. "I've known this dear, innocent girl since she was a wee child. I sewed for her family on her family's plantation in Baton Rouge. She hasn't had it easy, being on her own for the last seven years. Oh, I do hope life gets better for her."

"Do you want me to read her cards?"

"Are you feeling up to it? How is your back?"

"Better than it was before you took care of me. Get the cards."

Camelia went into Melba's boudoir and retrieved the cards off the mantle. "Here, *chere*. I'm anxious to hear about this misjudged child."

"Ah! Yes, I see what you mean," Melba said as she placed the cards in a three-card spread on her table. "She has had a big change from her former stable life. Separation from family. Dispersion of property. Sorrow. Tears. She has had to be very innovative to sustain a moral life and take care of herself under unusual circumstances." She pointed to The Three of Swords Card. "See here. I see a big misunderstanding."

Camelia's lips quivered. "Oh, heavenly Father in heaven. Why this child?"

"And that big misunderstanding did not end there. She has been misjudged and misunderstood by many, isolating her from the general public. See this Friendship Card here? She cherishes the few good friends that she has."

"Will this sweet girl find happiness or will she be alone for the rest of her life?" Camelia put her hand to her lips.

"She feels ostracized. Only after she feels acceptance, will she be able to find happiness. She is looking for true love, real companionship, and friendship. That means everything to her."

"Well, my family accepts her. We love her."

Melba swooped the cards in a pile. "I know you love her, Camelia. I didn't have to read that in the cards. I know you will help her to feel loved. Now, go to her. Do the marvelous thing that you do."

"I just love your shop, Katia. Your window display is very inviting with the lovely day dresses you've selected. I see that your exquisite taste shows up in the apparel. And the ruffled curtains you've added to the windows give an extra feminine touch to your décor."

"Do you really like them, Miss Camelia? I thought it would be good to have Theresa make up a few dresses to give the patrons an idea of what they'd look like. I have my sketches here, but it's not like the real thing."

"Excellent idea, Katia! Some people have no imagination."

"Thank you ever so much for agreeing to do the alterations, Camelia. I know how busy you are with your drapery business. Theresa is so busy filling orders, she doesn't want to stop to do small alterations."

"I love doing it for you, Katia. Besides, it gives me a chance to visit you. And I'd love to look at your sketches."

"I want you to give me some of your ideas. Look at this pillow-slip dress that Madame Broussard chose." The mauve straight-line dress hung from the shoulder to the hem. "She's the one coming in for a fitting after Eva. It's too long for her. And Eva has chosen this evening dress. She should be here any minute."

"I could have guessed this was the dress Eva chose. It looks like her. The little plumes around the neckline." Camelia held the skirt away from the hanger and fingered the fine velvet fabric.

"This is Eva's first dress purchase in my shop. She will select some clothes and recommend my shop to all of her friends. Oh, I'm so lucky to have such dear friends."

"Yes, you certainly are, Katia. Have you thought of hats to go with the dresses?"

"The milliner has been here with some samples, but I haven't ordered any hats yet." Katia looked out the window anticipating a customer.

A fourteen-year-old girl dressed in a sable brown morning coat bustled into the shop, the little bell ringing on the door. "Oh, how I wish you'd come back to the house, Mademoiselle Dubourg! I miss you! It's not the same without you."

"Why, Lottie?" Katia looked puzzled. "You've always told me you have a good clientele who never gives you any trouble."

"But it's the living conditions, Miss Dubourg. The woman who manages the bordello does not keep it clean like you did, and some of the women she's letting in to rent rooms are from the cribs. They bring the most unsavory men into the place. Can you come back, Miss Dubourg?"

Katia felt pity for the young girl. "Lottie, I'm afraid I can't do that."

"Even Caesar misses you. She doesn't even feed and water him like you did. He looks so shabby and dirty lately. I'm sure he misses you, too."

Katia softened at the thought of the loyal English mastiff who had protected her. But she knew she could never go back to that environment.

Lottie was practically in tears. "And they're using your flat upstairs for drinking parties. We've had the police come several times to break up all the roughnecks fighting. The wild parties are giving the bordello a bad name. Won't you please come back?"

Katia had never seen such begging eyes before. "Lottie, I'm trying to start a new life here. I have a business now. I can't go back. I just can't. I'm sorry."

Lottie's widened eyes stared back at Katia. For the first time, she looked around the fastidious dress shop and admired the beautiful dresses waiting for Madame Broussard and Eva. "Miss Dubourg. I guess you're right. If I had a beautiful dress shop like this and didn't have to deal with rats and drunks, I wouldn't go back either."

"There, there, Lottie." Katia embraced the young girl. When you save some money, you can leave that place and maybe start a little business of your own. See, I did it."

"You've always been so good to me, Miss Dubourg, even when I was late with my rent. Thank you for that anyway."

"Good luck, Lottie," Katia called out as Lottie left the dress shop. Katia looked back at Camelia. "My heart goes out to that little girl, Camelia. That could very well be me walking down the street when my father disowned me. Fortunately, I didn't have to deal with the men. Only rented rooms to the poor girls like Lottie."

"You've been kind to the child. You have a good heart."

Camelia and Katia looked through the dress shop window, eyeing the people walking by. "Oh, look who's coming down the banquette, Camelia. There she is. Isn't she just the most charming woman you've ever met?"

"She sure is," Camelia said, as she took Eva's dress to the dressing room.

Eva entered the shop, as the little bell on the door announced her. "*Bonjour*, mademoiselle. It's a glorious day when I can come to your dress shop and regard all of your exquisite dresses."

"*Bonjour*, Eva. Madame Arceneaux is awaiting you in the dressing room. She will help you into your dress."

Eva's face broke into a smile when she entered the dressing room. "*Chere*, what do you think of my new evening dress? Isn't it to die for?"

"Yes, Eva. It's exquisite. It exemplifies your flawless taste. Let me help you off with your morning dress." Camelia pulled the dress over Eva's head and hung it on a hanger.

"You do always say the nicest things to me, don't you now, Camelia?"

"Put your arms up. I'll slip this beautiful gown over your head."

The reflection in the looking glass stared back at Eva. "I do love the feel of this dress. All it needs is a little taking in over here." She slid her hands over the sides of her waist and admired the vision in the looking glass.

"Yes, this won't take but a few minutes for me to fix. You look absolutely ravishing in it, Eva. I'm so happy you're giving a bit of business to Miss Katia. I want to see her succeed with this dress shop. She's a girl all alone in the world."

"I'm more than happy to give her my business."

"Can you do one more thing for the sweet child?"

"And what would that be?" Eva looked up from admiring her dress.

"Invite her to your next fete. She doesn't get out at all. She needs to meet some new people."

"I'd be delighted to invite Miss Katia to my next fete. I've invited her to my plantation home for a little respite. I can't wait until she can get away from the dress shop for a few days. I want to introduce her to my cousin, Justice, who has a plantation home on the river road. He's quite the eligible bachelor."

"I knew I could count on you, my dear friend. Now, stand straight while I pin this up."

Chapter 26

He watched Katia descending the long, winding staircase, amazed at her gracefulness. Her delicate features and light complexion were exactly as his cousin, Eva, had described. He noticed her white satin pumps, as she daintily stepped down each step. Then, he looked up into her green eyes which matched the green evening gown she was holding up to avoid stepping on it.

The green eyes looked back at him in pure innocence. Vanity and seductiveness eluded her. Her pale lips were lips he suddenly wanted to kiss. He wanted to fulfill his wildest fantasies with her.

Her sweet voice woke him to the moment. "Hello," she said. "You must be Justice."

"You must be Katia." He felt like he was speaking to a vision.

She smiled in her demure way. "However did you know?"

My cousin, Eva, described you, but you're much more beautiful than I had pictured."

"Why, thank you, Justice, for the compliment."

"May I have the pleasure of escorting you to dinner?"

"I'd be delighted."

He offered his arm and escorted Katia into the drawing room where the other ladies were waiting for dinner to be announced. "I won't be very far. I'll be waiting to take you to dinner." He gave her a look of longing.

As Katia entered the drawing room, Eva's friends, who she had met at Eva's townhouse in the city, greeted her.

"Katia, how nice to see you again. Eva said you would be coming to the plantation. How lovely." Madame La Ferle rose and placed her cheek next to Katia's.

"Madame Godchaux, how nice to see you again." Katia walked to the sitting matron and bent to put her cheek to hers.

The old woman sat up straighter and looked very happy to have Katia join her. "I was so happy to hear that you'd be coming. Eva's told me you've been busy with a new business venture."

Katia sat next to Madame Godchaux and put her hand over hers. "It's so nice to be here and see the beauty of the country. And to see you again, too. Eva's friends always give me a lift with your wonderful hospitality."

"Oh, how I love to see a youthful, pretty face like yours. It makes me feel young again." Madame Godchaux giggled and nodded to Madame La Ferle.

From where Katia was sitting on the settee, she could see Eva welcoming Madame Chasse in the foyer.

Madame Chasse entered the drawing room. "My dear Katia, I am so happy to see you again. How have you been?"

Katia rose to greet Madame Chasse. "I've been very well, thank you."

"I hear you're living in the city with Eva."

"Yes, that's right. Eva's been very generous to invite me to her home."

"I've heard all about your new dress shop from her. I can't wait to come and see it."

"Please do come by for a visit. I have two expert dressmakers. Come and sit here next to Madame Godchaux." Katia moved to the end of the settee to offer Madame Chasse a seat and to better view the guests arriving in the foyer.

Katia spotted Antoine Friechet arrive with a younger man. She didn't remember meeting the younger man, but she remembered Antoine as the lawyer friend of her father, also the family lawyer in Eva's family. He was very kind to Katia, as she was growing up. She wanted to talk to him and ask if he'd seen her family.

As Katia walked toward the foyer, she witnessed Eva greeting her guests. "Monsieur Friechet, how nice of you to come."

"It's always a pleasure to see you, Eva. You're looking as ravishing as ever. And this is the guest I said I'd bring, my son, Geraud."

Geraud moved forward to kiss Eva's hand. "Well said, Father. I'm so happy to see you again after all these years."

Eva chuckled and took a step back to scrutinize Geraud, as she thought of their childhood romps. "Geraud, it's really you."

"My father's right. You do look as beautiful as ever."

Geraud's eyes crinkled up, and he grinned from ear to ear, as Eva touched the top of his hand.

Katia could tell that Geraud felt very attracted to Eva. Before she could approach Antoine Friechet, he retreated to a room on the men's side of the house.

Eva and Katia walked into the women's drawing room. "I believe you all know one another." Eva smiled to each of her guests.

"Oh, yes, *ma chere*. We're enchanted with your young friend," Madame Godchaux said.

A butler entered the room and announced, "Dinner is served."

"Shall we go in to dinner? The men have already been told that dinner is served." Eva led the way to the foyer.

The men stood waiting for their dinner partners. Katia saw Justice give her the eye and approach her. He held his arm out. She locked her arm around his.

Katia heard Geraud speak to Eva. "May I have the honor of escorting you, Eva?"

"Yes, Geraud."

Eva stood at the dining room entrance and welcomed each guest to her table with a gracious smile, as they entered the dining room. Antoine Friechet escorted the widow La Ferle at Eva's request.

Katia's gaze slanted over the dinner guests. She understood why Eva loved these people. Most were friends of Eva's parents and they had become her family. Eva loved to have these family friends in her home.

Katia noticed the fiery face of Geraud exuding emotion every time he looked at Eva, who was the perfect hostess.

Eva spoke to her guests, comforting them in every way possible.

Geraud looked into Eva's eyes, as he spoke to her. "You are the same, just as beautiful."

"I am the same except for a void in my life the last several years," Eva said.

"I hope to fill that void, Eva."

A wrinkle appeared in Eva's forehead. "You've married since I last saw you, haven't you?"

"No, I haven't married. I was disappointed in love."

"I'm sorry," she said. She looked down, looking for words of comfort, which she couldn't seem to find.

A servant filled the wine glasses, as another came with a platter of fish and served each person. Tati appeared after the fish course and placed two charred tomatoes topped with leeks and a generous slice of eggplant on Katia's plate and gave her a wink. Tati was always generous with Katia's favorites. The beef and lamb were served last with the warm breads.

Their aromas mingled with the jasmine and white roses on the table.

Katia peeked over the flowers. Justice's eyes twinkled in amusement across from her. "You look quite beautiful in the glistening candlelight. Not that you wouldn't look beautiful in the sunlight, I'm sure."

"Thank you, Justice. You're very kind."

"Eva tells me that you have a business."

"Yes. I started it recently."

"You're quite an ambitious woman."

"We'll see. This is my first business venture."

After dessert was served, Eva rose and led the women to the drawing room. The men departed to the men's chamber on the south side of the house for a smoke.

"May I talk to you later, Katia? I hate for this evening to end." Justice held his hand out to guide Katia up from the table.

"Perhaps later," Katia said.

"Can we go to the courtyard for a chat now?"

"I don't believe that would look too good for me to leave the ladies."

"Then later?"

"Yes."

As Katia joined the ladies in the drawing room, Madame Godchaux played a piece on the spinet. "Do you play?" Madame Godchaux asked Katia.

"Yes, I do."

"Do play something for us, *chere*."

"I don't think I play well."

"Do play something. Please," Madame La Ferle said.

Madame Godchaux rose from the spinet and patted the piano bench.

"Very well." Katia sat and played a piece.

She played two more pieces unaware of Justice watching her in the doorway. When she looked up, he backed away out of sight.

At the close of the evening, the ladies assured Katia they appreciated her entertainment. They walked to Eva's boudoir to get their wraps from the imposing armoire. The guests were bidding one another good night and making arrangements to meet again.

Justice pulled Katia aside out of the limelight. "I've been waiting all evening to be alone with you. Will you join me for a ride in the moonlight?"

"Now?"

"Yes, now. Why not? It's beautiful this time of night. I have blankets in the carriage. No need for getting a cape. Come with me." He grabbed her hand and led her down the main hallway to the back courtyard and around the house where his horse waited. As he helped her up to the carriage, the feel of her soft hand ignited him.

At the click of his tongue, the horse started up. The moonlight shone brightly, and the air was pleasant. He found no need to cover her with a blanket.

"You look just as beautiful in the moonlight as the candlelight." His eyes lighted on her and never left her.

He couldn't stop admiring her. He wanted this woman.

As a breeze came up, strands of her tawny hair blew across her face. He reached across to toss her hair away. His cold fingers glided against her cheek and they slowly found their way down to her chin and her neck.

"Where are we going?" she asked.

"This road off the River Road will give us a better view of Old Miss'. See there. It goes along the river." He pointed to the cool waves rushing in.

"Yes, it's quite beautiful. I've never seen it before at this late hour with the moon shining over it."

Her pulse leaped, as he stopped the carriage. She felt her heart pumping. He moved closer so that their bodies touched. She felt the warmth of his breath on her face and his arm around her neck.

His warm lips reached hers. He pressed her lips hard in a hungering kiss. She pulled back, her feelings ascatter, not sure if she wanted this man to kiss her or not.

"What's the matter?" he asked, disappointed.

"I didn't expect this. I haven't been with a man for a very long time."

"I think you're so very beautiful. I just want to kiss you. You don't mind if I kiss you, do you?"

"I, uh, guess not," she replied with hesitation.

His mouth found hers in a second, and his passion mounted. He pulled her toward him in a tight embrace. His hand curved around her breast and moved down beneath her dress and up her leg inside her bloomers.

As she felt his hand between her legs, she panicked. *He thinks I want him to do the unthinkable. Does he think I'm a loose woman? Oh, God, he thinks I would perform a sexual act. What has he heard about me?*

She pushed him back with all the strength she had and pulled the reins. "Giddee up!" She whipped the horse back to the River Road. Again, she whipped the animal until he raced at the speed that pleased her. When they reached Eva's plantation home, she stopped the horse and jumped off the carriage before Justice could assist her.

"May I help you?" he asked.

"No! I don't need your help. You think I'm a pros…"

"A what? No! I don't think…"

She rushed into the house.

He tied the horse to a hitching post and ran after her.

Running through the foyer, she reached the staircase.

She started up the stairs and looked down at Justice's look of horror.

"I'm sorry," he said, looking up at her. "I thought…"

"Yes, you thought I'd… And don't you follow me up!"

He turned to find his cousin, Eva, standing behind him in the foyer.

"I see you've made quite an impression on her, Justice." Eva's dark brown eyes sparked with annoyance.

He felt his face flush, as she briskly walked away from him. He heard anger in her voice, as he followed her into the drawing room.

"You've met Geraud. He's a childhood friend of mine, Antoine's son," Eva said.

"Ah, yes, Geraud," Justice said, trying to compose himself.

Geraud stood and shook hands with Justice. "Your cousin and I were reminiscing. We shared many good memories of our childhood. I was about to leave. Good night, Justice. Eva, good night. I can see myself out."

"Until tomorrow," Eva said with a smile for Geraud. She turned to face Justice with a stern expression. "And what am I to make of you and Katia? That was quite an entrance the two of you made." Her tone was sharp.

"Yes, I'm not sure what happened."

She gave him a doubtful look. "Justice, you know what happened. What did you say? What did you do?"

"Nothing to bring that on. I must admit I was quite smitten with her. We went for a ride. I told her how beautiful she looked. I kissed her and I…"

"You what?"

"I wanted to make love to her. I find her quite ravishing."

"Just like that, you wanted to make love—in the carriage?" She snapped her fingers at him.

"I just couldn't help myself. She looked so beautiful in the moonlight, in the heat of the moment, I just had to…"

"You had to?" She raised her voice. "Without even getting to know her or ask how she felt about you? You always act without thinking things out, Justice. This time, you've overstepped your bounds. I know for a fact, she's never been made love to."

"Not even with your former husband, Leonel?"

"Yes, not even with Leonel."

He looked at her inquisitively with furrowed brow.

"He was incapable of a sexual union. Even though he slept and bathed in every sporting house in the District, every prostitute testified at my annulment hearing that he was not able to perform a sexual act. And in six years, our marriage was never consummated. He was a monstrosity, looking for a fortune for doing nothing. His fortune hunting was the only thing that kept him busy, as he lived on the allowance I gave him for six years."

He sat, leaning forward, with his head in his hands. "I'm sorry you had to go through that, Eva."

He understood the cousin bond between them that encouraged Eva to mentor him ever since they were children. Usually, he took her advice. In this instance, he asked for it.

"I want to know more about her background."

"Her background is that she is the daughter of the most prominent lawyer in Baton Rouge. Leonel heard through my friends that Katia's father was looking for a legal assistant. He went to Monsieur Dubourg and lied about having a legal background. Monsieur Dubourg hired him and had him to his home. He met Katia and decided he wanted to be in that rich family, even though he was legally married to me at the time. The Dubourgs had no idea he had a wife in New Orleans.

Monsieur Dubourg soon found that Leonel had no talent for the law and dismissed him. Leonel told Monsieur Dubourg that he and Katia had performed an illicit act and that he thought they should marry. He wanted to benefit from their wealth. Katia's father was so incensed that his daughter would have an affair with such a disreputable man, he disowned her. He gave her a sum of money and told her to leave the home because she was a bad example to her younger sister and brother."

"And did she leave her home?"

"Yes, she came to New Orleans where she had some fond memories of coming here on holiday with her parents."

"Where did she live?"

"At first, she lived in a boarding house and tutored creole children. She worried about running out of money, because the money wasn't much."

"I can understand that." He looked intently, anxious to hear more.

"She wound up renting rooms to prostitutes in a bordello. She took the job because it came with a rent-free flat. The agreement was to just collect the rent and keep the place clean. She did not meet with the johns."

"Oh, I see." Justice winced, as he thought of Katia's hardship to be forced to take such a job. He bit his lip and looked away.

"She lived an isolated life for five years, not making friends or having a social life," Eva said. "When people saw her coming from the District, they assumed she was a fallen woman."

"How did you meet her?"

"She met up with Leonel on the streets of New Orleans, and he invited her to our home for a dinner party. He had a devious plan, as he always had. He thought that when she saw he was married, she would become his mistress, and her father would send them sums of money from Baton Rouge. Again, his plan failed."

"How so?" He scowled at the thought of another man taking advantage of Katia.

"Well, for one, Katia was supporting herself without the aid of her father and had become quite a business woman. When she realized Leonel was married, she was so embarrassed, she wanted to leave and apologized to me for coming to my home.

I could see that she was a young woman of breeding, and I knew that Leonel had lied to her. I convinced her to stay for dinner and we became friends—dear friends. Leonel was incensed at our friendship.

"Isn't it ironic? Some people look at Katia and me and see a fallen woman and a gay divorcee, when actually we're both virgins who suffered at the hands of the same man."

Justice saw pain through her smile. "I really think you should have told me this, Eva. Perhaps, I would have been more sensitive to her feelings. What can I do to make amends to Katia?"

"You can apologize for your unthinkable action and assure her that you respect her, and that it will never happen again. And that you would never do anything to hurt her. God knows that girl has been through enough."

"Has her father made amends with her?"

"Yes, Antoine Friechet, an old friend of her father's, invited him to my annulment hearing and everything came out in the open. Katia's father apologized to Katia in front of the court for believing a scoundrel and not her. He also invited her to return home to Baton Rouge."

"And?" Justice waited to hear of Katia's decision.

"She declined and decided to move from the District and start a small business. After my annulment, I invited her to live with me. She's filled my home with so much gaiety and happiness."

"May I come again tomorrow so that I may apologize to Katia, cousin?" He kept his face schooled to look directly at Eva with apology in his eyes.

"Come for tea at four."

Chapter 27

"Would you like tea or coffee, Geraud?" Eva turned from the sideboard to face him, and the memory came back to her of when she first knew him.

"Coffee, please."

She poured coffee from a silver coffee pot, walked across the room, and handed him a cup. His eyes met hers. She finally opened the gates of her past and remembered her first love.

"We have a lot of catching up to do, don't we, Geraud?" She sat across from him in a large wing chair.

"We certainly do."

"So, you've never married. And why not?"

"No, Eva. I've never married. I came close to marrying. We were both quite young and in love. Her parents had other plans for her to marry a wealthier man who owned much of the land here along the river road."

"I'm sorry, Geraud. Was it that young girl I saw you with at the opera?"

"I don't remember who you're referring to." He appeared deep in thought.

"I saw you several times with a young woman at the opera. Once, you introduced her to me. After seeing you many times with this young woman, I assumed you were betrothed."

"Did she have auburn hair?"

"Yes, with scads of red locks in the back—very pretty. Did you love her?"

A smile of recognition came to his face. "That must have been Genevieve, my mother's sister's daughter. And I did love her, but not the way you mean."

"Then, she was your cousin?"

"First cousin. Hardly one to fall in love with and marry."

"I always thought you married that girl." Eva thought back of how disappointed she felt when Geraud had introduced Genevieve to her, and she thought they were to be married.

"Well, now that that's settled, we can get to know one another all over again, can't we?"

"Yes, but promise me one thing."

"What's that, Eva?"

"That you won't throw sand in my hair ever again."

"Did I do such a monstrous thing?"

"Yes, you did." She laughed, and the pitch of her laugh rose higher, as he came toward her.

He pulled her off the chair and hugged her mightily. "Little Eva, I promise I will never throw sand in your hair ever again. Will you forgive me for such a terrible boyish prank?"

She couldn't stop laughing, as he hugged her tighter and tighter.

"Huh? Huh? Forgive me?" He leaned back and gazed into her eyes.

"Yes, I forgive you," she said with a trill in her voice. She heard a horse's hooves pounding up the road. "I wonder if that's Justice coming."

She glanced through the window and saw Justice on his horse, then heard the horse whinny at the men's entrance.

"He's come to see Katia." Eva retreated to the men's smoking room and opened the door to greet Justice. "I'm glad you could make it, Justice."

His face appeared hot from the heat of the day, and he looked preoccupied. "Where's Katia?"

"She's in the courtyard. Would you like to come to the drawing room for a drink?"

He brushed past her and rushed to the main hall of the house. "No, thank you, Eva."

He strode down the hallway to the courtyard to find Katia, embroidering, as she sat against a ledge. He walked to her and bent on one knee.

"My dear Katia, will you forgive me for my thoughtless actions last night? I do wholeheartedly respect you, and it will never happen again. I would never again do anything to hurt you. I'm hoping and praying, *ma chere,* that we can become friends and spend time together."

She continued to embroider and looked away toward the river. "I don't know if I could be with you right now."

"Oh, I see." He felt himself weaken at the thought of her not wanting to be with him.

He saw that she avoided his eyes. "We really got off to a bad start. Maybe you need time to forgive me. In a few weeks, I'm planning on coming into the city. I have a townhouse in New Orleans. I sincerely hope you'll soften your heart enough to let me take you to the opera." He rose from one knee and stood straight.

Her eyes did not meet his. "I do not foresee that."

"Dear Katia, don't judge me too harshly for being a man and falling in love with you. I found you so beautiful, I could not resist you." He left the courtyard in a hurry before he could change his mind and reach for her and kiss her once again, too passionately.

He rushed down the main hall, turned into the men's smoking room, and left by the men's entrance.

From the drawing room, Eva heard a door slam. "That must be Justice leaving." She ran outside to find Justice hurrying to his horse. "Justice, won't you come in for a chat? Geraud is here."

"No, I must leave."

"Not even for a few minutes? What on earth happened? Why are you leaving?

"I can't stay. I can't, cousin. Can't talk now." He turned his horse around and left.

She had never seen her cousin look so heartsick.

Chapter 28

Katia could tell that something brewed on Eva's mind that evening. Eva started a sentence several times and then stopped. "What is it, Eva?"

Eva set a vase with pink and purple peonies popping out on the dining room table. "I was just wondering about something, Katia."

"Yes?"

"Would you mind terribly if I were to invite Justice for dinner? I haven't seen him since we've been back from the plantation and he's in town. Oh, Katia, I can't just ignore him. He's my dear cousin."

"Of course not. You don't need my permission to invite your cousin to dinner. It's your home."

"But it's your home, too. I want you to feel comfortable here. And I would like for you to be with us when Justice joins us for dinner."

"You don't need me to be with you."

"Oh, but I do. I want you to be with us. And Justice would be most distressed if you were not to join us. He would not come here at all if it meant you would make yourself absent every time he were to visit me. I wish things were different between the two of you. I miss seeing him."

Katia looked across the table to see such petition in her best friend's eyes, she could not refuse her. "I will join you, Eva."

Eva ran around the dining table and hugged Katia. "I'm so happy, *chere*. I don't want to give either of you up. I want so to be with both of you."

Tati ran into the room. "Madame, Monsieur Justice is here. He's in the drawing room."

"Thank you, Tati. We'll go to receive him." Eva turned to Katia. "Shall we go in?"

"Well, I see you've planned this to the minute. You waited to ask me until he was in the house." Katia shook her head.

"Please, Katia. Don't be too hard on me. I'm in the middle of all this."

They walked across the hall to the drawing room, where Justice stood in front of the fireplace.

"Justice, I'm glad you could make it." Eva walked up to her cousin and put her cheek to his. He grasped both of her hands. "Thank you for inviting me, cousin."

He looked across at Katia, who stood frozen. "Miss Katia, I'm delighted to see you again and look forward to an evening with you." He walked over to her and reached for her hand. Holding it, he kissed it reverently.

"Justice." She nodded but couldn't find words to say to him.

Tati appeared and announced, "Dinner is served."

"Shall we go in?" Eva glanced at both of her guests.

Justice placed his arms around both of the women. "How lucky can one man be? I get to escort two of my favorite women in all the world."

They walked to the dining room and took their places at the table. Katia sat across from Justice.

Katia felt his eyes on her every time she peeked up. He would talk to Eva at the head of the table and watch her. At first, she thought he spoke to her and then realized he was speaking to Eva.

He looked across the table at Katia. "And what has been keeping you busy?"

Katia did not answer, thinking he was talking to Eva.

"*Chere*, what have you been doing lately?" He looked directly into her green eyes and waited for an answer.

"I've been very busy with my dress shop. It takes almost all of my time."

"No time for fun and relaxation?"

"I'm afraid not. Not when you're starting a business."

"Well, then. Tonight, you'll have to take some time out for entertainment. I've bought tickets for the opera. You do like the opera, don't you?"

"Yes, but I…"

"Splendid. We'll go tonight. The three of us. They're playing *La Cenerentola*. Rossini's comedy should take your mind off your work."

After dinner, as she left the table, she turned to Justice. "I really must beg off going to the opera. I have a very busy day ahead of me. I've several boxes of fabrics and trim I've not opened yet and several more being delivered tomorrow. They need to be unpacked and if they're wrinkled, I have to press them."

She turned to him in the foyer. "I bid you good night."

"You haven't forgiven me, have you?" He looked at her with penetrating eyes.

"Yes, I have. Haven't I told you how busy I am? I also have customers coming in tomorrow for fittings. I can't disappoint them."

"Then, I'll help you tomorrow. You certainly sound like you need help."

Katia raised her palms in protest. "Oh, no. You don't need to do that."

"I know. But I want to help you. A beautiful woman like you shouldn't work that hard."

"I'm really very tired. I must bid you good night. Good night, Eva. Have a good time at the opera."

Justice's face showed disappointment.

"Good night, Katia. I really wish you were going with us," Eva said

As Katia placed the Open sign in her storefront window, she heard the little bell announce her first customer.

"*Bonjour*," Justice greeted with a happy smile.

"Justice, what a surprise." She walked over behind a small counter and attempted a reasonable tone in her voice. "I didn't expect to see you here this morning."

"I told you that I would help you with your work."

"And I told you that you didn't need to help me."

"But I want to—really."

"I'm perfectly capable of running my business."

"*Chere,* please let me help you." He studied the dress shop and spotted a mannequin in a salmon-colored chiffon dress. "Your shop is quite elegant. But then I expected as much being that it's your dress shop. Where are the boxes to be opened?"

She pointed to a stack in the corner with reluctance.

"Do you have a knife or letter opener?" He peeked behind the counter, as she walked beyond the fitting rooms to the back room.

She returned with a sharp knife and placed it on the counter.

He slashed the first box open and pulled out two bolts of silk material—one in violet and one in pink.

Katia scrutinized the fabrics. "I believe the tissue paper preserved them well enough to keep from wrinkling. Thank goodness." She turned to see Justice had already opened another box.

He lifted another bolt of material and handed it to her. She touched the wrinkles on the beige linen material with dismay. "I think this needs a little pressing."

"Let me do it. Where is the iron?"

She looked at him dubiously. "I think not."

"You don't trust me with the iron?"

"Have you ever ironed?"

He smiled at her and lifted his shoulders. "Well, not really. How hard could it be?"

"Let me do the pressing lest we scorch brand new linen." She took the fabric to the back room to press.

When Katia returned to the front of the store, she found that Justice had created an efficient system of opening the boxes. "I see that you're getting quite good at this," she said.

"Most of the fabrics look good enough to put with the others on the shelf and don't need pressing," he pointed out.

"Yes, I see," she said, as she examined them. I'll take these to the other side of the store and place them on the shelf. These three fabrics need pressing. She returned to the back room to press the fabrics.

Soon, they formed a system of working together. Justice delighted in helping Katia. He loved being near her and watching her work.

When she'd walk into the shop to hang a dress, he'd watch her steady gait and admire the blond wisps of hair falling on the back of her long neck. He wanted to rush up to her and kiss her nape and turn her around and kiss her hard on her sweet mouth, but dared not.

Katia looked up at the cuckoo clock and rested her finger in her cheek. "You know, Justice, the customers usually start arriving at ten. I've got to get these boxes in the back room. They look a fright."

"Let me do that, *chere.*" He pulled the boxes to the back room where a dressmaker was pedaling away on a sewing machine, oblivious of him.

When he returned to the dress shop, Katia came toward him in a hurry. "Justice, I see a customer coming up the banquette. Please stay in the back room. If she sees a man in here, it may dissuade her from coming in. Please, go."

"Let me pull this last box out of the way." He grabbed the box and carried it to the back room while Katia impatiently watched him, ran after him, and shut the door.

She heard the little bell announce a customer and rushed to the front of the dress shop.

"*Bonjour,* madame," Katia greeted a little breathlessly.

"*Bonjour,* mademoiselle. I am looking to have a day dress made. Something simple. I would like to look at your fabrics."

"Madame, our fabrics are on this side." Katia placed several fabrics on the glass showcase counter.

"I see you have a very nice selection." She spied the fabrics and touched one daintily. "In the show case here, they are so elegant. My, oh my. I don't know if these are for me."

"They are the satins and laces for the bridal dresses, madame."

"I'm just not sure."

"I just pressed this lovely fabric that would make an exquisite day dress." Katia unraveled some of the beige linen material.

"This is linen, is it not?"

"*Oui,* madame."

"I don't know. I'm ever so hard to fit."

"I have expert seamstresses, madame, who sew for many notable women in New Orleans. They sew wide seams in all the dresses so that they can easily be let out for comfort any time you would desire a looser fit."

The customer's eyebrows lifted. "How clever of your seamstresses. I always have the tightness across here." She pointed to her hips. "If she can loosen a dress up any time I want, that would be wonderful."

"I've sketched some day dresses here, madame. You can have a look at them and see what you like."

The customer flipped through several pages of sketches and stopped at one. "What do you think, mademoiselle? Would this one be for me?"

"*Oui*, madame. This one is very nice. And this one here is simple elegance personified."

"Do you really think so, mademoiselle?"

"Yes, I do. You said you wanted simple. It is simple, yet elegant."

"It is rather nice, isn't it?"

"I think it would be very flattering on you."

"All right. I'll take this one—with the wide seams sewed in, of course."

"Of course. The dressmaker can be in tomorrow morning for a fitting. Could you make it at ten or eleven?"

"Yes, eleven would be convenient."

"*Bonjour*, madame, till then."

"*Bonjour*, mademoiselle"

There was a lull, and Katia went to the back room to press a dress. She found Justice, sitting in a chair, smoking a cigarillo. "Oh, no. Please don't smoke in here with all these fine fabrics. They will have a tobacco odor to them. Put it out."

"I'm quite sorry, *chere*. I didn't think of that."

The little bell on the front door announced a customer. "I must attend to my business now. Please, don't touch the iron in my absence." Katia hurried to the dress shop.

"*Bonjour,* madame. May I help you?" Katia greeted.

"*Bonjour*, mademoiselle. We've come for a ball gown for my daughter."

"Ah, yes. I have a book here with sketches of ball gowns. You can sit here at your leisure and look at them." Katia directed the mother and daughter to two comfortable chairs.

"Thank you, mademoiselle." They sat and perused the sketches with great interest. They went through the book and started over again.

"I keep going back to this gown, Mamma. Isn't it beautiful?"

"Do you really think it's for you?" she asked her daughter. "How about this one?"

"No, Mamma. I like these little rosettes on the bodice. It's just what I wanted."

The mother examined every detail of the style of the gown. "This gown may suit you, *chere*. We'll have to see what fabrics would go with this gown."

"The fabrics are on this side, madame and mademoiselle." Katia led the way.

Mother and daughter examined the fabrics Katia placed on the glass showcase. The mother went through all of the silk pastels. "Would you fancy this blue or this lovely pink, daughter? I rather like the pink."

"No, Mamma. I like this one." She pointed to the violet colored fabric.

The mother threw a sour look at her daughter. "That?"

The daughter's face broke into a smile. "It's just what I wanted, Mamma. I've seen pictures just like this in a catalogue in this very color."

"No, the color is all wrong for you. It would make you look old. You're only fourteen!"

"But I love it, Mamma."

"No. I'll not have my daughter dressed in a matronly color looking like an old maid. There'll be no gown in that color."

"Mamma, please!"

Justice listened at the door to hear the dilemma. He rushed into the dress shop. "Madame, please excuse me. Just this minute, we received this beautiful fabric in a splendid color. It's in the hue of apricots right from Mother Nature. It would make your young daughter look like the sweet virgin that she is. Would you like to hold the fabric up to her lovely face to see that it goes with her beautiful, young complexion?"

Katia saw the daughter look at her mother with pleading in her eyes. "Mamma, can I hold it up against me?"

"Very well."

The young girl held the apricot colored fabric under her chin. Her cheeks bloomed a peachy color and her blue eyes glistened, as she looked into the looking glass and admired herself.

"Your charm and grace stands out in that color if I must say so," Justice said.

"Thank you, monsieur." The young girl smiled in his direction. She turned to her mother. "Oh, Mamma, please, I really love it."

"Are you quite positive? Don't you want to look at others?"

"Oh, no. This is the one!"

The mother appeared hesitant. "When can she come in for a fitting? There's not a long wait, is there?"

Katia looked at her schedule book. "Tomorrow morning at ten, madame."

"Very well. We'll take it."

The daughter rushed to her mother in an embrace. "Thank you, Mamma. I will truly love this gown."

Katia caught the wink of Justice's eye. His lips parted in a grin at the pleasure of the young girl.

"Until tomorrow morning at ten, mademoiselle," the mother said.

"*Bonsoir.*" Katia made a little wave at the happy daughter.

"I know your daughter will be the most beautiful belle at the ball," Justice said, as he bowed to the mother and daughter.

"Why, thank you, monsieur. *Bonsoir.*"

"*Bonsoir,* madame."

When the women left the dress shop, Katia thought Justice looked quite pleased with himself.

Katia leaned back in a cushioned chair and let out a long sigh. "I hope that was the last customer. What a day. The hardest thing is getting a mother to pick a ball gown for her daughter. How did you know how to persuade her?"

"I wish I were able to do that with everyone." He walked to her and bent on one knee. "I so enjoyed working with you today, Katia."

"Thank you for your help. It was a busy day. I never would have had that apricot fabric unpacked to show it to that mother and daughter. And I wouldn't have made the sale. Thank you, Justice." Her lips curled up, as she looked at him.

"My pleasure. May I take you to dinner after such a hard day at work?"

She saw sad apology in his eyes. "Justice, this is one of those days when I want to go home and soak in a tub and go to my room and rest. When I have a busy day like today with two deliveries, Tati always sees how dead tired I am. She brings me a light dinner on a tray to my room."

"You still haven't forgiven me, have you?" He looked away from her. "Katia, I would never do anything to hurt you—or force myself on you. You know that. Don't you?"

She gazed at him without words.

"Oh, God, Katia, when I saw how beautiful you looked that night in the moonlight, my mind went wild. For a moment, I thought you wanted me, too. I know now—that's crazy."

For a moment, I thought I wanted you, too. Katia blinked and put her hand to her temple.

"I see that you're tired, *chere*. I'll take you home then."

Chapter 29

On a stormy night, Justice drove his carriage in a rush to Katia's dress shop with a heavy heart.

She looked up to him, as the little bell announced him. "I didn't expect you this evening."

"I didn't expect this evening's circumstances either." His expression grew grim.

"What's wrong, Justice?"

"Katia, Eva is ill with fever. Tati has been applying cold compresses most of the day. I've called a doctor. I think you'd better come home right away. These things come and go very fast."

She heard a sad crack in his voice. "These things? You don't mean…"

"Yes. Tati has seen yellow fever many times among her people, and she looks very worried. She has asked me to come and get you as soon as possible."

She dropped the dress she was holding on the counter. "I'll get my cape."

When they approached Maison de Catalina on Esplanade Street, two black servants, waiting for them, opened the wrought iron gates. They saw the doctor's carriage parked in the courtyard. Justice knocked on the north side of the house where the ladies entered into Eva's boudoir.

An imposing door opened to find the doctor peering out at them into the darkness. "You can't come in here. Yellow Jack here! Go to the other side of the house."

They heard a terrible retching sound and Tati's voice saying, "Come on. That's okay, Madame Mommie, come on."

Katia peered to see Eva's long, black hair hanging over a large, porcelain bowl that Tati was holding before the doctor closed the door.

Katia looked up into Justice's sad eyes and saw her fear mirrored in them.

He led her to the men's side of the house through the rain. "Let's go this way. You should get out of your wet clothes and change. I'll wait for you," he said, as they entered the house.

"What about you?" she asked.

"I'm not sure what to do. I'll wait a bit and see if they need me for anything." He wrung his hands as he spoke.

Katia went to her room and changed into warmer clothes and a shawl. Returning downstairs, she heard voices coming from Eva's boudoir. She listened at the door and thought she heard Justice's voice. *Had he gone in there when the doctor had told them not to go in her room?*

She opened the door a crack. The smell of burnt hay hit her nostrils. She crouched down to see Justice, sitting in the far corner of the room, as he leaned over to hear Eva's weak voice say, "You're executor of my will, Justice. There's an account for the servants and a special account for Tati." Eva's voice cracked, and she coughed, as her body shook violently.

"Don't talk, *chere*. It stresses you," Justice said.

"If you will no longer be able to keep her on, give her the money. She only knows this house."

"Yes, I know, cousin. Please try to rest. I won't abandon Tati. I know her mother died at birth in this house and you cared for her as a baby as if she were your own. I know how much you love her," Jutice reassured her.

Eva's body writhed, as she looked across the room at him, her mouth moving with no sound escaping but a rasp. Then, the words came out clear. "Let Katia live here. Please."

"Rest assured, my dear cousin, that Katia will always have a home and so will Tati. I will see that Katia is always taken care of. I would never dream of asking her to leave. I love her, cousin."

"Oh, I'm glad, Justice. Now leave me lest you get this scourge!"

"I can't leave you, Eva. I can't."

The doctor threw his gloves on the floor. "Justice, perhaps you should go for the priest. I have given madame everything I can to make her comfortable. Tati will continue to apply the cold compresses to try to get the fever down and feed her cold fluids. I've shown her what to do."

Justice's face dropped, as he rose with hesitation. "Do you really think it's time?

"Yes. This usually lasts from three to six days. She will either break the fever or... I think it best you get the priest at this point. We just don't know." The doctor removed his white cotton robe and face mask and threw them on the floor. He slipped out quietly through the outside women's entrance.

Justice opened the boudoir door to find Katia standing just outside.

Eva turned her sweaty head, unable to lift it from her pillow, to see the hazy outline of Katia standing in the doorway. "Do not come in. Don't catch this scourge!"

"But Eva, I want to help you. What can I do?"

Katia watched Justice walk past her with an ashen face and shaky hands. "You'd best stay out of that room, Katia." He closed the door to shield her from the contagious disease that loomed the air in the boudoir.

"What is it? Is it really yellow fever?" Katia asked.

"Yes. To think my dear little cousin may... I never thought I'd be getting the priest for her. This is my worst nightmare."

She heard a sob in his voice. "Oh, I'm so sorry, Justice. I feel so helpless. Is there something I can do?"

"The best thing you can do is to stay healthy for me, my love. Otherwise, I see no reason for living if I were to lose you, too."

She watched him walk unsteadily down the hall and turn to leave the townhouse with a mournful heart.

Katia turned to see Tati leaving the boudoir with a pan of water and some wet cloths over her shoulder. "Oh, Tati, can I help you? Where are you going?"

"That's okay, Miss Katia. I'm going to get more cold water to cool Madame Mommie off."

"Let me go with you. I can help." Katia followed Tati, as Tati walked swiftly down the main hall and across the courtyard to the kitchen. In the kitchen, they found two pans of cold water on a large table. Tati threw down the wet cloths and retrieved several dry, clean ones off the table and threw them over her shoulder. Two black servants picked up the wet cloths and left the room.

Tati picked up the pan of cold water and started to rush off.

"Can I take this other pan of water, Tati? Then, you won't have to come back for it," Katia said.

"If you want to, Miss Katia. But I can come back."

Katia followed her back into the main house with the pan of cold water. When they reached Eva's boudoir, Tati turned to Katia. "Miss Katia, you can set that pan of water on the floor near the wall. Madame Mommie Eva said I am not to let you in her room under no circumstances lest you catch the fever."

"But what about you?" Katia asked with fear for Tati.

"Don't matter about me. I have to try and get madame cooled off and that's all I got to do. My *Tante* Lana told me before she died that my whole job was to take care of madame." Tati entered the boudoir and shut the door quickly.

Katia returned to her room and lay down to rest but could not sleep. She went back downstairs. Opening the boudoir door a crack, she saw the priest anointing Eva with oil on her eyes, ears, nostrils, lips, hands, and feet. He prayed, "May the Lord pardon thee whatever sins or faults thou hast committed."

In the stagnant heat of imprisoned air, candles illuminated Eva's dying face, turned yellow, with eyes closed. Beads of perspiration rolled down her yellow cheeks. Her black, matted hair looked wet against the white pillowcase.

Justice prayed out loud in a cracked voice. "Oh, God, please, please, please spare my dear cousin and take me instead. I will never ask for another thing in my life if you spare my dear cousin."

The white-gloved priest straightened and looked across the room at Justice. "I am through here. May she rest in peace." He left by the outside women's entrance.

Katia closed the door and drew a deep breath. She suddenly felt weak and sat on the floor. The death scene sickened her. She placed her head between her knees and meditated.

My best friend is going to die, and I am all she can think of at her time of death. And Justice. He has so much love in his heart for his dear cousin and for me. He says he loves me. No one has ever said they loved me like he has. And he thinks of my safety also. I've always wanted a man who could express his love for me. That's all I ever wanted. These are the best friends I have ever had, and they may die. There's nothing I can do to save them. Show me a way. Please Lord, don't let Eva die and don't let Justice catch the yellow fever. I think that I love this man.

The next day proved horrendous, waiting for death. Katia closed her shop and paced the halls of Maison de Catalina. She tried to help Tati, but there was very little that Tati did not do herself. Tati feverishly worked day and night without stop to try to cool Eva's body. The iceman chipped away at the ice block and delivered crushed ice at Tati's orders. She kept applying the ice to Eva's body, kept ice in Eva's mouth, and kept feeding her cold liquids.

Justice stayed at the townhouse, refusing to leave Eva's side to rest. He could not be consoled by Katia or Geraud, who paid visits to the house. When they expressed words of sympathy, he would walk away from them, as if in a trance, not being able to comprehend what was happening.

The feeling of death seemed to permeate the walls of the house. Katia heard Eva cry out in the night, "Justice!" She saw him rush to her room and followed him.

He entered Eva's boudoir. Opening the door a crack, she wanted to hear what Eva wanted.

"Justice, make it legal." Eva's voice sounded muffled, as she strained to get the words out.

"What, *ma chere?*"

"It must be drawn up in a will or they will not believe Tati." She lifted her flushed face from the pillow, straining to breathe.

"Do not exert yourself, cousin. Try to keep calm."

"Go to Friechet now. He must write my will. Tati to receive Maison de Catalina. Have him record it. Also, say Katia can live here as long as she wants. Bring it back. I will sign." Eva's sunken eyes fell deep into her cheekbones ringed by bruised half moons.

"You can trust me to carry out your will, Eva." He left the room with his heart torn in two. He brushed past Katia in the hall. "I have to go to Friechet's office to carry out Eva's last will."

"Now?" Katia asked.

"Yes. By the time I get there, his office will be open. It's important to her, and now it's important to me."

Katia went to her room, but could not sleep. She knelt at the side of her bed and prayed that the scourge that had entered this house would leave, and her friend would live.

Please, God, let Eva live.

Nighttime turned to morning, as Katia waited for Justice in the drawing room. The stillness in the house felt like quiet death creeping in.

The whinnying of the horses outside broke her stupor. She looked out the window and saw Justice jump from the carriage. She felt herself get excited at the sight of his tired face.

"Justice, I'm in the drawing room." She was too weary to get up.

He entered, looking more haggard than when she first saw him through the window. "How is she?" he could only seem to get out. He collapsed in a soft chair.

"She made it through the night. That's all I know." Her sad green eyes met his.

"I'll go to her," he said.

"I need to speak to you, Justice."

"I'll be back as soon as I give Eva the will."

He went to Eva's room and read the will to her.

"I am pleased," she said. She coughed, and vomit spewed from her mouth.

"It's okay. It's okay, Madame Mommie. I wipe it all up," Tati said.

Eva managed to sign her initials on the will with the aid of Justice's hand over hers. "Rest now, *chere*. Just rest, and I'll return."

Returning to the drawing room, he found Katia sleeping in a chair. He gently touched her shoulder to waken her.

She opened her eyes to find Justice looking at her with tired, admiring eyes.

"You wanted to speak to me?"

"Oh, yes, Justice. I've been thinking and praying, and I have an idea for Eva."

His eyes lighted. "What is it?"

"I have a friend who is knowledgeable about herbs. She was a nurse during the War Between the

States and is now a midwife. I want to ask her if she has an herb for the fever. She treats new mothers for lots of things, and I suppose they get fevers, too." She looked at him for approval. "I know it's just a chance, Justice, but I have to try every chance I can for her."

"Of course. Where is this woman?"

"She lives in Faubourg Marigny—not far."

"Can you call her?"

She noticed the first sign of hope in his eyes. "Yes, I can. Well, I can reach her by her neighbor's telephone who lives across the hall from her."

"Let's do call this woman by all means."

They walked to the breakfast room at the back of the house, facing the courtyard. A small round table sat in front of tall windows with a view of a fountain. Katia hurried to the wall telephone. She picked up the earpiece and spoke into the phone. "Operator. I want to call Faubourg Marigny. The number is Faubourg 1283." She looked at Justice with hope.

"Hello, Madame Le Doux. This is Katia Dubourg, a friend of Madame Arceneaux's. We have a friend, Eva Villanueva, who has the fever and I desperately need to talk to madame. Is she in?"

"Hello, mademoiselle. Yes, I remember you, the pretty young woman from Baton Rouge. Madame has spoken of you many times. I think she is sewing this morning. I'll go and knock on her door."

Katia could hear Madame Le Doux knocking on Camelia's door. *Knock. Knock. Knock. Knock.* "Camelia, it is your friend Katia on the telephone. She says she desperately needs to talk to you. Her friend, Eva Villanueva, has the fever."

"Oh, Mon Dieu!" Camelia's voice carried through, as she ran to the telephone. "Hello, Katia. What is it, my child?"

"Oh, Miss Camelia. I'm desperate. Eva has got the yellow fever. Do you have an herb for that?"

"Oh, Lord in heaven. Can you come over right away? I'll give you everything I have. I can't leave the children."

"Yes, I can."

"I have one herb I give my daughters when they get a fever and it breaks within twenty-four hours. We can try it. I have another one to stimulate the immune system. We can try that. And there's another one. Oh, I'll look for it. Can't think of the name. Come as soon as you can. Just come."

"Thank you, my friend. I will come right away."

She turned to Justice, who stood by her side, listening intently. "She said to come right away. She'll give me everything she has that may help her."

"I'll take you. Do you know her address in the faubourg?"

"Yes. Twenty Ten Burgundy Street."

Chapter 30

As soon as they reached Camelia's house, Katia jumped from the carriage and ran to the front door without waiting for Justice.

Camelia opened the door before Katia could knock. "Oh, come in, *chere*." She embraced Katia. "How is she?"

"Not good. I am scared, Camelia. I fear she will leave us. I won't be able to bear it if she dies."

"I know what you're feeling. I've had that scared feeling, believe me. Let's just concentrate on the herbs for the moment. We'll pray for her after we get the herbs to her. One is yarrow, and I've put it in this here envelope and marked it with the directions. You brew a tea in boiling water. Then, cool it down on the ice block for a while. She can drink a little at a time."

"Oh, thank you, Camelia. You're always so good to me. How can I ever repay you?" She started to cry and quickly wiped her eyes. "How selfish of me to think of myself at a time like this. Oh, my friend, Eva's cousin, is here. Can we let him in?"

"Of course. Do come in, monsieur, to my humble home."

"It's a pleasure, madame. Katia has told me what a wonderful friend you have been to her since childhood. My name is Justice Villanueva. I am Eva's cousin."

"It's so nice to meet you, but unfortunately, under the most dire circumstances. I've given Katia here the yarrow herb with directions written on the envelope. Another one I have works on the immune system and fights infections. It's really a cure-all herb that should alleviate the fever. I have written the directions on the envelope—one to two grams of dried root to one cup of boiling water. You will make this the same way I told you to make the yarrow tea, Katia. And here is an envelope with red raspberry leaves. It works for so many illnesses. I'm never without it. It's for her fever, nausea, vomiting, and the black diarrhea. The herbs work well in conjunction with one another."

"Thank you, madame." He gave her a look of gratitude.

"There's this other herb I've been looking all over for, but I don't seem to have it. I haven't used it in years." She put her hand to her forehead and bit her lip. "I remember using it once. It's a very strong herb. Oh, it's...it's... The name of it. I remember now. It's baptista," she said with a relieved smile.

Justice looked at her seriously with bloodshot eyes.

"Where can we get it?"

"It seems to me the only person that had any, and she gave some to me, was Dago Annie. I saw her shake a fever out of a dying woman in postpartum. That woman can raise the dead, I swear. She saved my daughter's life from hemorrhaging. Yes, she did." She nodded, affirming what she just announced.

"Can we call her?" He asked with a tired voice but full spirit to help his cousin.

"Annie doesn't have a telephone. People just go to her home when they need her. Or you walk in her neighborhood and chances are you'll see her walking with her black bag from one house to another in Frenchtown to deliver a baby."

"Let's go to her," Justice said, as he turned to leave. "Do you know her house?"

"Yes, she's at Eleven eighty five Governor Nicholl." Camelia followed Justice and Katia to the carriage, and he assisted them.

"I'm so happy that Madame Le Doux was able to take care of the children so that I could go with you," Camelia said.

As they crossed over to Frenchtown, they turned on Governor Nicholl Street to find Annie's house. Katia noticed several people walking from the French Market with bags of produce and fish for their lunch. She felt hunger pangs when she saw the apples and melons poking from the bags, as she hadn't eaten in over a day but dismissed it.

"Are we near her house yet?" Justice turned to Camelia.

"No, this isn't her street yet. Oh, look there," Camelia said.

"Where?" He didn't see anything unusual.

"I'd recognize that coat anywhere. I sewed that coat for her. Annie!"

Annie turned her hefty body around to see who called her.

Camelia waved and held herself back from standing in the carriage. "Annie!"

"Wait until I stop, madame. I'll help you down," Justice said. He assisted Camelia from the carriage, and she ran to Annie.

"Oh, Annie, we need you desperately. A dear friend of ours is sick with yellow jack. Do you have that herb?"

"Which herb, Camelia?"

"You know that one called baptista. I want to give it to my friend, Katia, to give to our dear friend, Eva. This is the third day, Annie. We have to hurry or it will be the end for her."

She pointed to her house. "Come to my house up here. This way. I will have to show them how to make this tea. It's very important to use just the right amount. I will have some instructions for them. I'm on my way to deliver a baby. We have to hurry." Annie started swiftly toward her home.

Camelia waved for Katia and Justice to follow her.

They followed Annie down a gangway across a courtyard and up a squeaky stairwell to an old slave quarter flat.

Annie rushed into her flat and left the door open for the others. She unlocked a tall, free-standing cabinet and shuffled through shelves of envelopes and bags from one shelf to the next. Reaching to the back of the cabinet on the bottom shelf, she pulled out an envelope marked with a large black X and brought it to her kitchen table.

"Come in," she said, waving her guests into her sparse flat. "Sit down. All of you. This baptista is a strong herb, mind you, but it's your last chance to save your friend. You must listen to me and follow these directions I am writing down for you. Make the tea in boiling water, and then cool it down on an ice block to stop the black vomiting and bleeding. Only one teaspoon at a time. Watch not to make it stronger than what I say on these directions lest you cause her more black vomiting and diarrhea.

Take bed sheets, fill them with ice, and wrap her in the ice filled sheets until she cries of the cold. Place bits of this root in her mouth. But ignore her screams for mercy until she is cold and rid of the fever.

If the fever breaks, take her away from that room right away and cleanse her body with this herb. Then, burn the blankets and mattress, the rugs, the drapes, everything in her room to get rid of that damnable disease."

"Oh, thank you, my friend, for the valuable advice." Camelia kissed Annie's hand.

Annie pulled away. "That's all I can do for you, I'm afraid, except I want to give you this special amulet for your friend, Eva. Put it on her altar and pray for her to get well. I put a special herb in it. I add this special herb of mine to my amulets for sickly people. They always get healthier." She handed it to Katia.

Katia turned to Camelia. "She already has an amulet on her altar. Remember, Camelia, you gave me one to give to her."

"The amulet I gave you for Eva was for her to learn to trust a man. This one is for her health," Camelia said.

"I have to rush off to deliver a baby, a new life." Annie's voice brightened at the mention of a new life. "*Bonjour*, madame, mademoiselle, monsieur."

Justice rose and placed several dollar bills on the table upon leaving.

Annie's eyebrows lifted, as she spotted the bills. "*Bien,* monsieur. You are most generous."

"You are the generous one, madame. You walk with God."

Eva screamed in horror, "Stop! Stop it! Go away!"

Justice wrapped her in the sheet of ice and rubbed the ice crystals firmly against her body. Katia aided him in cradling the sheet on the other side of the bed.

Eva's eyes shuttered with pain and her lips quivered. Justice's narrowed gaze would not leave her tortured face. He grabbed for her hand and rubbed it. "Please, hold on, *cherie*. And drink this wonderful herb. Please." He held a teaspoon to her lips and fed her the herbal tea a teaspoon at a time.

As the ice crystals melted, he ordered more ice, and Tati went to the kitchen to retrieve more. Two servants returned with Tati and poured the ice over Eva's body.

Justice chipped away at the herbal root and placed it in Eva's mouth. She gagged.

"Please don't spit it out. I beg you. Keep it in," he said.

Her tormented eyes asked, "Why?"

"I want to keep you alive. Please!"

He continued to rub her body with crushed ice, traveling up to her cheeks, nose, sunken eyes, and forehead.

Anger warred her face. She snarled at him. "Why are you doing this to me? Stop! Stop it!"

"I just want to keep you alive."

"I can't! No more!" She screamed in agony. "Oh, God, help me!"

He let go of the sheet and knelt beside her bed. "Lord, please spare the life of my dear cousin. I am begging you."

Tormented screams echoed through the once silent halls of the house. The servants came running and listened at her closed boudoir door.

Her lips continued to quiver without sound. Her body writhed in pain, as she let out a guttural moan. His cold hand squeezed hers, as her body jerked. Pain twisted her face, as her breathing quickened. "Please! Oh, please," she screamed. "Let it end!"

Fear simmered in Justice, as he watched his cousin in pain. He winced and called out. "Katia, what are we to do?"

Katia walked over to Justice and knelt next to him. She put her hand on his shoulder and embraced him. They held on to one another for a long moment.

In a calming voice, Katia spoke tenderly to Justice. "I know this is not easy for you, Justice. We must do what Annie said. Just keep icing her and feeding her the herb. It is hard to do, I know, but we must ignore her screams. Oh, God, I don't want to think of what could happen."

"You're right, Katia." He nodded and harrumphed. He stood and resumed rubbing ice crystals over Eva's body against her cries and moans and continued through the entire day and night. Katia stood by his side, aiding him with holding the iced sheet over Eva and feeding her the herbal tea on a teaspoon.

They continued the ice treatments into the fourth day.

In the late afternoon, out of exhaustion, Katia and Justice fell asleep on the hard, cypress floor outside of Eva's boudoir door. The decaying odor like rotting hay reeked from the space under the door, filling their nostrils, as they fell asleep.

Evening came, and the hall was dark. Tati's voice woke them.

Katia looked up to see Tati, standing still before her. "Did she d…?" Katia gulped and could not get the word out in a cracking voice.

Justice's eyes opened wide in a state of shock unable to speak and afraid to ask.

Tati appeared ready to faint, holding back a sob, steadying herself against the wall.

"Madame is cold."

Chapter 31

He looked down into her death-masked face, tinged yellow, sunken eyes closed. She lay in a pool of ice water, her jet-black hair floating away from her above her head and alongside her cold body.

"Oh, my God!" He touched her white arm, a lifeless glacier. The glacier moved! And the shuttered eyes opened! "Eva!" he bellowed. "Eva! Can you speak, *ma chere?*"

Her lips quivered, but she could not speak, except with her eyes. Those pain-filled eyes that told him that she was still alive stared back at him.

"You don't need to speak. Just blink once to let me know you are still with me."

The sunken eyelids blinked but one time and closed

Justice fell to his knees and held his hands in prayer. "Thank you, God. Oh, thank you, my God. I promise I will do everything to serve you."

Katia let out a cry and moved closer to the bed. "Eva, we are here for you. We will help you to get well."

Justice threw off his shirt and kicked off his boots. He saw Katia's wide-eyed look of surprise. "We must act quickly. I'm taking Eva upstairs to your room, Katia. I want you and Tati to cleanse her with the baptista herb. Then, put one of your clean shifts on her and throw her nightgown out to burn. I will go to my town house, just two blocks up Esplanade, and burn these britches and bathe myself. I will return to take her to my home until she gets well."

Katia looked disturbed. "Must you take her away from us?"

"Yes, Monsieur Justice. I will miss madame. 'S my job, you know, to take care of madame Eva," Tati said.

"I want both of you to bathe while I am gone and put clean clothes on and burn the ones you've been wearing. When I return, I will take both of you to my home to care for madame. I will have the servants burn everything in Eva's room as Annie instructed us. They'll also wash the walls down in the house and burn everything that's come in contact with us."

"But I don't have…" Tati looked confused.

"Tati, put your Sunday gingham dress on after you bathe. I will get you more clothes later. I promise. You will be with madame at my town house. Everything will be the same, except you will be at my house instead of Madame Eva's."

He lifted Eva out of the pool of ice water in one loud swoosh and strode in long barefoot steps out of the room. Going up the stairs, he carried his cold cousin in his bare arms. When he got to Katia's room, he kicked the door open and laid her on the bed.

Katia and Tati rushed to keep up with him. When they got to the top of the stairs, he was on his way down.

"Pack a bag with the things you will need. I will be back for all of you," he promised.

"Eva, how are you, my dear?" Katia looked down into Eva's solemn face with eyes barely open.

"Madame Mommie Eva, I'm here to take care of you," Tati said.

"I... No strength... If Justice hadn't carried me up... I don't know how..." Eva had strained to speak. Words eluded her. She closed her eyes.

"Don't worry about a thing. You'll get your strength back soon," Katia said.

"I'll get some nice broth for you, Madame Mommie." Tati started to scurry out of the room.

"No, wait, Tati. Come. Hold my hand." Eva looked at Tati in her Sunday Sabbath dress, as Tati came near.

Tati walked over to Eva and sat on a chair next to the bed. She looked down at her with grateful eyes.

Eva reached for her hand. "Tati, I want to thank you. I know it wasn't easy for you." She coughed, as she tried to speak. "You waited on me hand and foot. How could I ever repay you, you sweet child?"

Tati waved her hand with a smile. "Aw, Madame Eva, no need to praise me. It's my job to take care of you. And because I love you."

"Tati, you. Pretty today. Your best dress. What is the occasion?" Eva asked.

"That you are getting well! And look Madame Eva. Did you see this fancy petticoat table here? Every time I walk by it, I can't help noticing myself in the looking glass with those flowers etched all around it. And Madame Eva, I'm in a pretty room right next to yours. There's a little crystal bell right here on the table next to your bed. Now, any little thing that you need, you just ring that bell, and I'll be right here."

Katia walked around the boudoir and admired the beautiful furniture. "This room is lovely, Eva. I've never seen such an exquisite duvet. The hand-embroidered border must have taken someone a year to do. You're certainly in beautiful surroundings to recuperate."

"Yes. Justice. Very generous. His mother's boudoir. My aunt. Fine taste. Always loved her room. Never thought I'd stay in it." Eva coughed and turned on her side.

"I'm going to the kitchen to get you something to drink, Madame Mommie, and some hot broth. Tati left Eva's side with a happy face.

As Tati opened the door to leave, Justice walked in with a bouquet of roses. "These just came in for you, Eva."

"Flowers?" Eva didn't have the strength to lift her head.

"Yes. They're from Geraud. He asked if he could see you, but I took the liberty of telling him that you are not quite ready for callers. I want you to regain your strength." Justice placed the bouquet on the night table.

"I see there's a card in the roses. Do you want me to read it, Eva?" Katia peered over Eva, waiting for an answer.

"Yes, please Katia. Read." Eva's eyes remained closed.

"My dearest Eva, I so missed seeing you during your illness. I will try to be patient during your convalescence and look forward when I may call on you and resume our friendship. With deepest respect, Geraud."

Three weeks later...

"Now, just one more stair to go. I told you that you could make it, Madame Mommie Eva. Come now. You're doing very well. Come sit here." Tati led Eva to a cushiony chair in the drawing room.

"Thank you, Tati. I don't know what I'd do without you," Eva said.

Tati started to plump the cushions. "These cushions look so old and beat. They've seen their day."

"They are old. My aunt and uncle built this town house in 1866 when my parents built theirs. Those cushions are probably that old." Eva let out a smile.

"It's so good to see you smile, madame." Tati noticed something red sticking out from under the cushion. "What is this?" she asked, as she pulled it out.

"That's the chair Monsieur Justice sits on. Oh, it must be." Eva fought back a laugh.

"What?" Tati noticed that Eva looked pleased.

"Oh, just place it back under the cushion and don't breathe a word of it to anyone."

"Why is that, Mommie Eva?"

Eva placed her index finger over her lips. "I'll tell you later, Tati. Just put it back and don't tell anyone."

Tati replaced the red satin amulet under the cushion and smiled.

They heard the horses outside, and Tati went to answer the door at the men's entrance. "That must be Monsieur Geraud, calling on you."

As Tati opened the door, Justice walked in. "Good evening, Tati. Is Katia in the drawing room?"

"No, monsieur. Madame Eva is in the drawing room."

"*Bonsoir*, Eva. How nice to see you up and about." Justice kissed Eva on the cheek. "You look quite well. Is Katia home from the dress shop?"

"Yes, she came home quite fatigued from a full day. She's up in her room. Tati just went to get a tray to take up to her."

"I regret that I couldn't help her today. I had to take care of some problems at the plantation. Please, excuse me, cousin." He abruptly left the room.

Tati walked toward him with a tray to take up to Katia. "Let me take that up to Miss Katia's room, Tati," Justice said.

"Are you sure, monsieur?"

"Yes, I'm quite sure." He took the tray from Tati and walked swiftly up the stairs.

Tati returned to the drawing room in a happy mood. "Ah Hah! Something is up, Madame Eva. Something is up." Tati giggled, as she pranced around the room. "Something is finally happening in this old house. I can feel it."

"Katia?" He stood behind her boudoir door with a hammering heart.

"Yes?" She wondered if she heard right.

"May I bring your tray in to you?"

"Why, yes."

She came to the door to find him standing with her dinner. "Do come in," she said politely. She wore a white shift with short sleeves that displayed her thin arms.

He walked across the room and placed the tray on a table next to a comfortable chair. "Please, have your supper. May I just sit here a while? I'd like to talk to you. You don't have to talk. Please, eat and have your warm tea. You've had a busy day, I've heard."

"Yes, I've been quite busy. I don't know where these women bought their clothes before I opened my dress shop." Katia sat next to her supper and reached for her plate.

"I so enjoy having you and Eva in my home, even if I don't see a lot of you, Katia."

"We truly appreciate your hospitality. Eva has recovered slowly but surely, so I've been able to return to the shop."

"I wish I were able to spend more time with you."

She tilted her head and looked at him with question in her eyes. "We see each other daily."

"Yes, but we're always with other people in the room. I want to spend time alone with you—to become intimate with you. Does that displease you? I must know."

"It does not displease me." She drank her last bit of tea and looked up at him.

He knelt at her feet. "That's all I wanted to know, *ma cherie.*" Taking her hand, he held it in his and kissed it.

"I've been wanting to kiss you for such a long time. There's never been a good time what with Eva's illness and Tati running in and out. May I kiss you?"

She looked into his violet eyes and saw love and apology in them, brushing her hand across his raven hair. She thought of his caring ways with his cousin, and how he had desperately worked to keep her alive. And how he kept her away from Eva, protecting her from catching the vile disease. She nodded with a smile.

He stood and reached for her and picked her up from her chair. Holding her close, she felt his hungering lips against hers. Then, his lips traveled her cheeks, eyes, and forehead. "I can't stop," he said. "I want to kiss every part of you. I want to marry you."

At first, she stiffened at the shock of what he had just announced. But then he kissed her into relaxation, and the soft kissing sounds lulled her like chamber music. Her jasmine scent permeated the air and soothed them both. She didn't even realize that he inched her toward the bed.

"Do your feet hurt from standing all day?" he asked.

"A little."

"Let me massage your feet, *chere.*"

She sat on the bed, as he massaged her feet and relaxed her. "Does that feel better?"

"Mmmm. Yes."

He held her foot and kissed her toes one by one and in between.

She giggled at the new sensations in her feet. Taking the other foot, he kissed her toes one by one and traveled to her ankles. "You have the most beautiful ankles, *ma chere.*"

He kissed her ankles reverently, and she gasped. "Why, I never had…" She lay back on the bed and enjoyed his lips on her ankles and shivered.

"I know, *ma chere.* You've never had your ankles kissed like this. Have you?"

"No, I never."

He pushed her dress up. "And you never had your knees kissed before, have you?" She looked down at him, as he kissed her knees.

As his lips found her thighs, she wiggled and started to moan. He kissed her thighs with more passion. "And you never had your thighs kissed before, have you?"

"No," she barely let out.

"I didn't think so," he said with a smile. "But such a beautiful woman like you should not miss having her body kissed all over." His deft hands traveled to her groin with a soft massage until she whimpered. "Do you want more?"

"Yes," she breathed.

"Tell me, *chere*, tell me what you want."

"I want mmm......" She gasped as her body quaked to his touch.

He kissed her groin, pressing his tongue into her warm flesh. He moved up to her belly and kissed it and tongued her belly button.

She held in breath and wiggled her toes, as she arched her back.

"Oh, I almost forgot. I was distracted by your beauty. Did I ask you to marry me?"

"No, you didn't."

"Will you marry me, ma cherie?"

As he tongued her belly button, she screamed in delight, "Yes!"

His fingertips running up and down her belly created delicious shivers up and down her spine. The tiny hairs on the back of her neck rose up until she could feel them burning. The burning feeling ran down her back and around her body landing on her hardened nipples. She suddenly noticed his fingertips on her nipples. She whimpered from the fiery sensations running through her body.

He cupped her breasts and massaged them. His tongue went to her hardened nipples, and he sucked until she cried out. She loved the tongue-like attention he gave her breasts. It made her feel warm and loved. The warm feeling went down to her female passage, wanting him.

"I do love you, *ma cherie*. You know that, don't you?"

Her heavy breathing did not allow words to leave her mouth, as she quivered. She moved her head up and down as their eyes met.

He kissed her lips openmouthed and teased her with his tongue to open hers. She opened her mouth to him and felt hardness against her body.

"You've never felt this before, have you, *ma chere?*"

"No, I've never felt that before," she whispered.

"No one has ever wanted you as much as I want you," he whispered in her ear. He kissed every valley and crevice of her body with his moist lips. The warmness of his lips pulsed against her labia. Her female petals swelled, as his tongue found its way inside and went in and out, in and out.

"Oh!" she moaned. "Oh, I never."

"You never felt this sensation before, did you?"

"No, I never."

"Do you want me to stop?"

"No!"

Her mons tremored for him, as she squirmed on the bed.

"Tell me you want me to love you," he uttered.

"I want you to…"

He tongued her female lips, wet and ready for him. His tongue went in and out of her until she canted her hips. He stopped and slanted her a look of desire. "Oh, how I love you!"

He locked into her wet warmth and pushed until she screamed in delight. Her sparkling eyes looked up to his. "Oh, I never…"

"You never had this before, did you?" His gorge glided in ecstatic movement of her body.

"No. Never!"

"I know, my darling. I want to love you from now on. Will you love me too?"

"Yes, *cher.*"

Her body shuddered and her eyes flicked up to him, as she pulled him close to her body.

He felt pleasure that she had reached her plateau. He continued to fill her with his gorge and move in and out of her body until he reached his climax.

They held one another in the stillness of the evening.

"I don't want you to leave my house, *ma chere.* My life would be empty without you. Will you stay?"

"I will stay," she said.

"Even if Eva returns to her home?"

"We'll probably be married before Eva returns to her home, won't we?"

"Yes. When would you like to be married?"

"Very soon. Week after next."

"Parfait, ma amour."

Rosalia
Wants Love

Chapter 32

"How lovely of you to have me for afternoon coffee, Rosalia." Katia eyed the lovely tapestries in Rosalia's sitting room.

Rosalia poured coffee into a cup and handed it to Katia. "It's so nice to have you, Katia. How is Eva feeling?"

"She's getting stronger every day, thank God. Justice was at her side the whole time she was sick. He's such a caring person."

"I'm so happy. Give her my best regards."

"I will, Rosalia. Now tell me all about it. I can't wait to hear." Katia bounced in her cushiony chair with eyes wide open.

"What?" Rosalia gave her a questioning look.

"Oh, you know. Don't make me ask all of the intimate questions. Tell me. About the first time."

Rosalia felt mystified, not knowing what to answer. She looked across the room and sipped her coffee.

"Oh, how insensitive of me. It's rude of me to ask such a personal question. I should have realized you don't like to talk about such things, and that's you. It's okay. But I have to tell you, Rosalia, how utterly wonderful it was for me. It didn't hurt nearly as much as I thought it would."

"It didn't? Really?" Rosalia was taken aback.

Katia didn't notice the surprise in Rosalia's manner.

"No, truly. It didn't. He was so gentle and so loving, kissing my body in every place. He started with my toes. It was delightful."

"Your toes?" Rosalia laughed, as she almost gagged on a bite of crumpet.

"Yes, my toes. Oh, don't laugh, Rosalia. It was delightful. He started kissing my toes, then my ankles and thighs, and then, well, he kissed me everywhere." Katia let out a little giggle. "I didn't think I would ever want a man as much as I wanted him. He kissed me all over and massaged every intimate part of my body. And to my surprise, I wanted him. I honestly wanted him to make love to me."

"And did he?" Rosalia asked.

"Uh huh." Katia looked down into her coffee cup and a smile spread across her face.

Rosalia shifted uneasily in her seat. *How I wish I could feel the way Katia does. I wish I could enjoy my husband holding me in bed, naked, and wanting him the way Katia wants Justice. And having Elmo make love to me, kissing every part of my body and really enjoying it. Oh, that would be the most wonderful thing in my life.*

"Oh, Rosalia, I finally found true love. It was so wonderful to have someone tell me that he loved me. I never thought I would hear those words from a man I also care for.

"He said that he doesn't want to go on without me and can't imagine not having me to make love to. He asked me to marry him. Rosalia, I'm going to get married!"

"I may not always seem very responsive to you, Katia, but I am truly very happy for you." Rosalia rose to embrace Katia.

"I'm going to have my family at the wedding. Can you imagine? After all this time, I'll be reunited with my sister and brother who will be witnesses at my wedding, and my father will give me away to my husband." Katia stopped and looked across at Rosalia's sad-eyed expression. "I'm sorry, Rosalia, if I became too personal with you."

"Oh, no, it's quite all right."

"When I think about when your mother gave me that amulet to put under a cushion when I'd meet the man I wanted to marry, I never believed that would happen. But it did!"

"My mother gave you an amulet?"

"Yes. She gave it to me one night at her home. I think you were out with Elmo that evening."

"Oh, I didn't know about that. Mamma never mentioned it." Rosalia remembered the night Elmo wanted her to set their wedding date. He had wanted her to kiss him, but she was very cold to him.

"You know, Katia, you've done me a great favor by telling me you wanted him. I wasn't sure if it was all right to enjoy a man. My sister never told me about her first time, and I never asked. I've felt guilty for certain feelings I've been having for Elmo. He's such a dear, you know, so patient with me, and now you've dispelled my guilt."

"Guilt?" Katia looked at Rosalia with raised eyebrows. "You should never feel guilt for loving someone."

"I didn't really know what I should feel. I never discussed my feelings with anyone. When you told me how much you enjoyed him kissing you on every part of your body, well, you've cleared up a lot of things in my mind. I like that you told me you loved him kissing you everywhere."

Katia embraced Rosalia. "My dear, innocent friend. I truly pray that I was of some comfort to you, whatever it was. If you ever need to talk these delicate matters over with a friend, I am here for you."

"Mamma, you gave an amulet to everyone except me. Why?"

"Well, Rosalia, you weren't home the night I gave amulets to my dearest friends and your sister. You were out with Elmo at a dance. And with a dear, sweet man like Elmo, I thought you had the world in your hands and didn't need anything."

"Oh, but I do!"

Camelia heard a plea in her daughter's voice she had not heard before. "Is there something you want to tell me, *chere?*"

"Nothing in particular, Mamma. But we all have needs, don't we?"

"Why, yes. Do you want me to give you an amulet now?"

"Yes, I do." Rosalia nodded firmly.

Camelia got up from her sewing machine and rushed to her armoire in her boudoir to get a red satin pouch. She returned to her dining room and rummaged through the small side drawers of her sewing machine to grab a spool of red thread and a needle. "I've got to get the herbs from the pantry." She went to her pantry and chose several jars of herbs off the shelf and dropped a pinch of each into the red pouch. "Oh, and one more, the catnip. Well, one more, the bergamot. That makes thirteen. We can't have more than thirteen."

Rosalia stood behind her mother. "What's the catnip for, Mamma?"

"It prevents colds and fatigue. And also prevents premature births and miscarriage. We can't have that." Camelia winked at her daughter.

"And the bergamot?" Rosalia asked.

"It protects against harm. I also put love potion number nine in there for extra measure."

Rosalia followed her mother to the dining room. "I'll stitch the fourth side of the amulet, Mamma."

"Very well. Now, remember, put this little pouch in your marriage bed, and whatever it is you're praying for, I'm sure God will grant it to you. But you have to believe in what you're praying for. I think I might know what you and Elmo are praying for."

Camelia gave a pleasant wink and nod to her daughter.

Rosalia looked up from her tiny stitches. "I'm ready to have a baby, Mamma. I want to have a family with Elmo."

"That's wonderful, Daughter. I can't wait to be a grandmother and have a little precious one to love."

"I know, Mamma. And what do you want? We've all said what we want, but you've never breathed a word."

"Oh, I don't know." Camelia winced.

"Come on, Mamma. I can tell something's on your mind."

"Well. I think it's about time I stop mourning Claudio. I would love to get rid of this burning loss I've been feeling for too many years—since Collette was two."

"I think so, too. I'll get an amulet for you from your armoire."

"For me?" Camelia felt surprised at the thought of sewing an amulet for herself.

Rosalia rushed back to the dining room with a red satin pouch. "Now, let's go to the pantry and pick some herbs for you."

Camelia chose three jars and dropped a pinch of each herb into the pouch.

"Tell me what you're using in your amulet, Mamma. I want to learn from you."

"Sandalwood powder, sage, and anise. Some load stones I have here. Some mint for protection, some wood betony for warding off the bad feelings and loneliness and illness, a pinch of ambergris for protection from bad luck and some pokeweed to purify my blood. Nine is enough. Has to be an odd number."

Rosalia took the red pouch from her mother. "I'll stitch the one seam up for you, Mamma." She walked to the dining room, and Camelia followed.

"I never even thought of making an amulet for myself, Rosalia. Funny, you should think of making one for me, baby girl. Wouldn't hurt, I guess."

Rosalia sewed the last little stitch. "You put this under your pillow, Mamma. And believe what you ask for will come true. Now, say what you want out loud."

She sighed and gazed at her daughter with watery eyes. "I pray that it's time for me to stop mourning my dear husband, Claudio, after seventeen years."

Chapter 33

Elmo sensed that Rosalia was restless that evening and wanted to get away from the family. She gazed at him as never before, as if she had something to tell him.

"Is something wrong?"

"Not at all. I just want to be with you this evening," she whispered.

"Oh, is my little wife missing me in the daytime?"

"Yes, Elmo. It seems you spend more time away from me, than with me."

He walked her to the boudoir and retired to his study where he'd wait until she undressed and got into her nightclothes. When he returned to the boudoir, she appeared from behind the dressing screen, wearing her trousseau nightgown. He took in her beauty and turned the kerosene lamp dimmer.

In bed, he started speaking softly in her ear while caressing her. His calming voice seduced her. He spoke in whispers that passed from lips to ear with barely a sound spoken, slowly and sweetly. She caught each sweet word and responded with kisses on his mouth and ears. The sweet whispers excited her more than anything he could physically do.

The more he wooed her, telling her he loved her, the more she wanted him and the feel of his soft skin against hers. The sound of his mellow voice stirred something inside of her. She couldn't resist his soft mouth that spoke so tenderly to her. She realized she wanted him.

"Elmo, could you take my nightgown off?" She looked into his eyes, as she never had before.

"Why, of course, *ma chere.*" He gingerly placed his fingers at the bottom of her gown and pulled it up over her head. His eyes followed the small shapely breasts he had never been allowed to touch. Her brown nipples looked serenely untouched. She was his innocent bride.

His thoughts suddenly took him back to the time when he was fourteen years. His father had taken him to a legalized brothel in the District to introduce him to his manhood.

Upon entering a room in the brothel, a prostitute lay in bed naked, a steely look in her eyes. Her harsh voice startled him.

"Come here, boy, but take your clothes off first."

"I don't want to take my clothes off," he remembered saying.

She let out a coarse laugh. "You're a real novice, aren't you now? Well, come here anyway. I can work with your clothes on. Come on. I won't bite you. Are you afraid of me?"

"No, I'm not afraid of you." He walked to the bed to get a better view of what a prostitute looked like. He didn't like what he saw. She looked hard, not old, but hard.

"Come on. I haven't got all day," she urged.

`She pulled him up on the bed. "How do you want me? On top of you or on the bottom?"

Her acrid body odor had not set well with him, and the unfamiliar smell of hashish permeated the room.

"I don't want you," he said. "I don't want you at all!"

He ran out of the room, left the brothel, and waited outside for his father. His father frequented the brothels in the District, a habit he detested, never understanding the attraction to those slovenly women who made their bodies available to every man who walked into the brothel. He never returned to a brothel again much to the chagrin of his father.

His friends' fathers did the same as his father. They felt they had to indoctrinate their sons in the business of sex. Unlike Elmo, his friends quite enjoyed sex in their teens.

Elmo looked to his bride, an innocent girl, who never gave herself to any man. She was exactly what he wanted—a girl who only loved him. A girl who wanted to please him, but wasn't sure just how to do it.

His bride pulled him to her naked body. "You have been the most patient man. I think we have waited long enough as husband and wife, don't you, *mon cher?*"

"You have been worth waiting for, my sweet wife. And *mere* keeps listening at our door every night for some excitement. Let's not disappoint her tonight." He smiled at his wife with love in her eyes.

"I'm so new at this, but I want to love you like you want to be loved. I am so sorry I've made you wait this long.

He covered her mouth with kisses. "Kiss me back," he said. "Just love me. No need to explain."

She kissed him with passion and moved her hands to his chest and rubbed it gently. Her hand moved down his groin and rested. He placed his hand on hers and moved it down to his loins. She felt the firmness that Katia had told her about and held him midstaff.

He moved her hand up and down the hardness.

"I want you to kiss me first—everywhere," she whispered.

His mouth went to her neck and breasts and to her stomach. He kissed between her legs and caressed her thighs, while his hands smoothed her legs.

"Are you ready for me to make love to you?"

"Yes, *cher*. I am ready for you."

He massaged between her legs until the moistness he was waiting for was there. He rubbed her bush until she quaked and entered her slowly. "I will try to be as gentle as possible, my sweet. Does it hurt?"

"No, it doesn't yet, but I will not worry about it, if it does."

"Please, let me know. I want to know if I hurt you."

She held him tight. "I am willing—for what I put you through."

His warm breath feathered her cheek. She started to move her body to his thrusts, as he went in and out. She had to please this man who loved her, who'd waited until she was ready to be a woman.

He looked down into her eyes with love. In a breathless voice, he asked, "Is it good for you?"

"Yes, it's good for me." She moved with his body, but she was not ready for that passionate gasp a woman has at the end of her high plateau. She did not know what wondrous thing could possibly lie ahead.

His strokes became harder and faster. He saw pain in her eyes and the furrows in her forehead and felt grateful that she didn't ask him to stop. His thrusts were fast, and he couldn't stop now, even if she asked him.

"*Mon cher,* I love you. I don't tell you very often, but I do love you," she said.

"Oh, my love, I can not hold back. I… "A shiver went down his spine, as he came and looked at her with apology. "I am sorry, *cherie.*"

"Sorry? For what? I thought it was the most wonderful thing I could ever experience with you." She kissed him with warm lips and caressed his body.

"It was?" He laughed and held his cheek to hers. "Some day, my dear wife, you will enjoy our lovemaking as much as I enjoy it. I promise."

He heard footsteps outside their bedroom door. "I think mamma is pleased tonight," he said.

"Why is that?" Rosalia asked.

"She was at the door, and I'm sure she heard the bed creaking with our lovemaking thrusts."

"Tomorrow night, can we go to the *garconniere,* as we did on our wedding night? That was so lovely with your friends serenading us, and make love there?"

"If you wish." He looked at her with laughing eyes and told the woman, who thought she was plain, how beautiful she was.

Easter Sunday

Chapter 34

Andre and La Fonda attended six a. m. Easter Mass in the hospital chapel. The altar candelabrum and the devotional candles in front of the communion rail illuminated the dark, cold chapel. The Sisters of Charity in white habits sang Latin chants, as they walked in a steady gate down the aisle, two by two, their white veils trailing behind them.

La Fonda looked up to Andre with admiring eyes, as he mouthed the words of the chant in order to not draw attention to himself. Her heart felt aflutter. She couldn't wait until mass was over, for today was the day she would be discharged from the hospital, and they could live in the new flat that Andre had rented for them.

She knelt next to her husband and watched him pray piously with eyes closed. A priest entered the sanctuary and started mass. La Fonda could not keep her mind on the significance of the ceremony. She could only think of Andre and her children loving her and kissing her in their new, warm home. *Oh, but I can't let the children kiss me lest they catch my terrible disease. And I can't kiss them either. And I can't kiss Andre!*

As the priest preached the gospel of Easter Sunday, La Fonda wondered how her children must have grown. She felt a void in her life from the last year that she had not lived with them. *How my children must have changed! Will Blossom remember I'm her mamma?*

She heard the words of the priest. "You seek Jesus of Nazareth, who was crucified. He is risen." The nuns sang joyously, "Alleluia! Alleluia!" This time, Andre couldn't stop himself from singing out the words, "Alleluia! Alleluia!"

He closed his hand around hers. Her heart thumped with joy, as they left the chapel to gather her things up in her room. She would finally leave this lonely place and return to her young family.

They caught the trolley and headed for the French Market to buy fresh oysters and French bread. When they approached the seedy part of Frenchtown, La Fonda pointed to a man through the trolley window. He was lying on the ground. "Oh, look, Andre. Why is he lying in the dirt?"

"Pay him no mind. He is lying in front of the tavern. He's probably had too much to drink. We won't get off in this part of town. We'll get off at the French Market to buy our breakfast."

Andre helped La Fonda off the trolley while he carried her burlap bag with her few belongings. "Come, *chere,* we'll buy some plump oysters."

Upon seeing the chickens and ducks, hanging by their feet next to ropes of elephant garlic and smelling the freshly caught fish in barrels of ice crystals, La Fonda's breath caught for a second, and she giggled. "I forgot how much fun this place is. Look, Andre, at all those ruby red tomatoes."

"Yes. We'll buy some," Andre said, as he walked over to the fruit peddler

La Fonda laughed with pleasure. She walked backwards, as she held Andre's hand, trying not to miss the sights of the papayas, bright oranges, limes, and pink grapefruits lined up in boxes half-wrapped in red tissue paper. The carp and haddock peered at her through glass cases openmouthed with eyes bulging. "Look, Andre. They look like they're staring at us." She pointed to the freshly caught fish with eyes shining in their direction.

"Some of those fresh oysters, please," he said. He watched the merchant scoop handfuls of oysters into a bag. "That's fine," he said, as he reached for the bag. He turned to La Fonda. "I know you love them, don't you, *chere?*"

"Oh, yes, Andre. I haven't had fresh oysters since... Oh, lookie here, that big catfish with those long whiskers."

"Yes, he's sure a big one. Let's get some tomatoes and fruit for the children."

"Well, those are sure delicious looking tomatoes and mangoes. And the bread smells so good, I can hardly wait to eat it." She sniffed the bread, as he stuffed it into the burlap bag.

They walked outside the open-air market, then headed for the trolley stop and waited. He looked at her tired face and decided to take a carriage and raised his hand as he saw one coming in their direction. "Come, La Fonda, we'll ride this carriage."

"But can we afford it?"

"Yes, we can afford the carriage, but I can't afford for my love to get sick again. Come, *chere.*"

As they boarded the carriage, she turned to him. "Andre, you're just too good to me. You'll spoil us."

"That I will." He grinned in her direction.

"Where is our new flat?"

"You'll see. It's walking distance to *Tante* Camelia's in the faubourg. That is, when you're well enough to walk. For now, until you're strong, we'll take a carriage. But first, I'll take you to our new home."

"Oh, I'm so excited. I can hardly wait to see it."

"It's just a few more short blocks, and we'll be there."

"Andre, this neighborhood looks so nice. The children will love it."

"We're coming to it, La Fonda. It's that second house from the corner. See, that gray one across the street. This is it, driver."

He tapped on the window, and the driver stopped.

"Oh, my Lord. It looks so nice. Even has flowers in the front." She put her hands to her mouth to stifle a cry.

Helping her off the carriage, he looked at her grateful face. He paid the driver and led her to the front of the house. "Looks nice, doesn't it, La Fonda?"

"It's beautiful!"

"Well, we have the back flat, and it's downstairs. We don't have to climb steps any more. The landlady lives in the front flat alone. She's very quiet."

"It sounds too good to be true, Andre."

He set the burlap bag down and carried her into their new home. "Oh, Andre. This is so exciting. You've never carried me before."

"I didn't do this when we married. This is a special occasion. I feel we should celebrate our new home together."

As her legs touched the floor in the kitchen, she screamed with excitement. "Andre, I love this kitchen. And we have a bigger table. Wherever did you get this nice table?"

"Compliments of *Tante* Camelia. She said a tenant left it in the attic and never came back for it. We didn't have room for it in our other flat."

"And a pantry. I never had a pantry before." She walked into the narrow room lined with shelves and placed her hands across each shelf, as if feeling a precious piece of silk.

They walked ahead to another door, leading to a bedroom. Twin-sized beds lined two walls, and a crib lined a third wall. "This is the children's bedroom," Andre said.

"Oh, my. And they've each got their own bed. This is so nice, Andre."

Beyond the children's room, they came to another bedroom with a double bed. "This is our very own bedroom, where I will make love to you, *chere.*" He looked at her with glistening eyes.

"Oh, Andre. I don't know what to say. It's all too-too good." She spied the bed with the powder blue chenille bedspread, staring back at her. The urge to lie down on the bed came over her.

As if he read her mind, he pulled the bedspread back to reveal a plump duvet. "You lie down, La Fonda, and rest. It's been quite a jaunt for you this morning to ride the trolley and carriage. I'll come and get you when breakfast is ready."

"Do I look that tired to you, *cher?*"

"You look beautiful to me, but you mustn't overtire yourself. Rest a while. We've a full day ahead of us. *Tante* Camelia wants us for Easter dinner at one p. m. Rest, *amoureux.*"

She lay on the bed. He kissed her gently on the cheek and left the room.

She could hardly believe her good fortune, as she drifted off in a dreamlike trance. Eyes closed, she tried to imagine the children, not having seen them in weeks.

Before she knew it, he touched her arm. Her eyes met his smile. "La Fonda, are you ready for breakfast?"

"Oh, yes. I can hardly wait to eat that nice fresh bread."

"Let me take you to see the rest of the flat." He helped her out of bed and led her to the dining room. "See, we have a lovely dining room just like *Tante*

Camelia. We'll get a dining room table as soon as we save up for one."

"Oh, that'll be lovely. We can have *tante* over for dinner, and Collette and Rosalia. Oh, my."

They walked through the dining room, smelling of freshly painted walls. "This is our parlor. We've yet to get furniture for it."

"It's so nice, Andre. And I see there's another entrance in the parlor."

"Yes, now let's eat."

They walked to the kitchen where her eyes spotted the table laden with fresh oysters, sliced tomatoes, and mangoes. "Oh, my goodness. This is an embarrassment of riches. I never did see the likes of a breakfast like this. You sure didn't diddle to fix us the nicest meal ever."

He pulled out a chair for her. She sat and marveled at the food. "What would you like to start with?" he asked.

"That French bread I've been hankering for."

He sliced a piece of bread and handed it to her. "Now,

have some of these plump oysters." He dished up several oysters on her plate along with tomatoes and mangoes.

"This is so delicious, Andre, I can't tell you. Oh, and that coffee smells like it came right from heaven." She sopped the bread in the oyster liquor and ate ravenously.

"I'm so happy that you're eating, *ma chere*. I want so to get you well and strong. You haven't always eaten very much this past year, and I've been worried about you."

"Well, I didn't have food like this in the sanitarium. You know exactly what I like, my sweet husband."

"Have some more coffee. And would you like more oysters?"

"I couldn't eat another bite." She rubbed her belly and sighed. "I want to save the oyster shells for the children to play with. They'll love them," she said, as she gathered the oyster shells in one pile.

"Now, let's rest awhile until we leave for *Tante* Camelia's." He gave her a long look.

"Oh, I can't wait to see the children. Can we leave now?"

"No, my darling wife. I've been waiting for you for over a year. I need some alone time with you. *Tante* is busy preparing Easter dinner, and you'll have the children the rest of your life." He led her to their boudoir and closed the jalousies. He eased her down into their bed atop the plump duvet.

Her eyes sparkled in excitement, as she looked up to him. "Are we really together again?"

"Yes, we are, *ma cherie*. You haven't forgotten how to love me, have you?"

"Oh, no, I haven't, Andre."

"Tell me like you used to. Tell me to love you."

She looked up to him with a question in her eyes.

"You know." He winked at her, as he leaned in closer to her body. He saw the remembering glint in her eyes and fondled her neck.

"I want you to love my breasts, Andre. I miss you kissing them."

He removed her blouse and brassiere. "You mean like this?" He tantalized her nipples with his lips, pulling on them until she squealed.

"And love my belly, too," she let out breathlessly.

He lifted her skirt and moved to her belly and kissed it, then pressed his tongue hard into her navel, moving it back and forth, in and out.

"Ohhh," she moaned.

He moved down her body and removed her bloomers. His warm hands brushed her thighs up and down, and he kissed between her legs.

"I missed you so much. I never thought we'd be together like this again," she whimpered.

"Don't spoil this by crying, La Fonda. Be happy."

"I am happy. Oh, Andre, I'm so happy to be here in our new home with you, you'll never know."

He rubbed her bush and pressed his gorge against it. "I can't wait any longer, La Fonda. I've wanted you for so long."

"I can't wait for you no more either." She moved and quaked to his movements, as she hungrily kissed him and pressed him into her body. He glided into her, and they soon resumed their old rhythm.

"Oh, God. I don't know how long I can hang on. You feel so

good, La Fonda."

"*Mon Dieu,* Andre! I shouldna kissed you. You could catch tuberculosis from me."

"I don't care. Kiss me again."

Chapter 35

"Mamma, I've never stopped putting the amulet that you gave me in our marriage bed. And now…"

Camelia looked up from the steaming gravy pot and asked, "And now? What, Collette?"

"Persistence has paid off. I'm going to have a baby, Mamma."

"Oh, Daughter, I knew it would happen for you." Camelia turned to witness the happiness in Collette's smile. "It's the best news I've heard in a long time." She stopped stirring long enough to embrace her daughter. "I can't stop whisking this gravy or it'll be lumpy."

Gossie bounced into the kitchen with Geetie and Blossom behind him. "When is my mamma and daddy coming? When, *Tante?*"

Camelia looked down at the children. "Your mamma and daddy should be here any minute."

"I want my mamma," Blossom said with a tearful look.

"Oh dear. Get Blossom away from this hot stove lest she burns herself. Gossie, take your sisters to the parlor and sit in the front window and wait for your mamma."

"Is mamma really coming today?" Geetie asked.

"Yes, yes, she's coming today. Go and wait for her with Gossie and Blossom."

Gossie grabbed Blossom's little hand. Blossomed screamed in protest. "No. I want mamma."

"See. She won't come, *Tante.*"

"Go to the window, Blossom, and wait. You'll see when your mamma comes to see you. Tell her a story, Gossie."

"About what?"

"Tell her a story about your mamma. Tell her how pretty your mamma is and how she came clear across town just to see her." Camelia winked at the boy. Gossie shrugged. "Come on, Blossom. I'll tell you a story about mamma."

"Oh, someone's at the door. Can you stir this, my sweet, while I receive my guests?"

Collette took the whisk from her mother's hand, and Camelia ran from the kitchen to the front door. "Oh, Rosalia and Elmo, what a delight. And Lily, so nice to see you on this Easter Sunday."

"Happy Easter, Mamma." Rosalia squeezed her mother in a tight embrace.

"Please, come in and make yourselves comfortable. Dinner's about ready." Camelia peeked through her front window, pushing a lace curtain aside. "Oh, I see my friend, Melba, and her boy, Silas, comin' up the banquette." Melba walked with more ease than Camelia had seen her walk in years. Silas strutted proudly with his mother's arm locked in his.

Camelia waited for them on her porch. "Oh, what a lovely sight this is, Melba. You walking to my home on an Easter afternoon. You haven't walked up here to my house in thirty years." Camelia let out a happy cackle.

Melba grinned a full smile. "I know, my friend. Ain't it great? I can walk to your house now, if Silas helps me."

Melba took the stairs slowly, while Camelia waited at the top for her. As Melba took a rest on a step, leaning on a banister, Camelia encouraged her. "Come, sweetheart, you can make it. Come on. Do you want me to help you?"

"No, *chere*. Just let me catch my breath. I can make it."

Silas nudged his mother's back. "Come, Mamma. I'll help you." He gave her a gentle push, and she climbed the next step.

After a few respites, Melba reached the landing. "Happy Easter, Camelia. How good of you to have us."

"Oh, do come in for our Easter celebration, Melba. Silas, you look dapper today. Come on in."

Silas smiled and tipped his hat toward Camelia. "Thanks for the invite, Ma'am."

"Melba, come in and meet my good friend, Lily. And you haven't met my daughter, Rosalia, have you? And her husband, Elmo, Lily's son.

Elmo rose to offer a seat. "Please, do sit here, madame."

"You've heard me talk a hundred times about my good friend, Melba, haven't you, Lily? The one that reads the cards. We go way back."

"Oh, yes, indeed. I'm so pleased to finally meet you, Melba. And Silas, I've met you here before, always helping Camelia around the building."

Silas removed his hat and held it at his side. "Pleased to meet you, ma'am."

Melba rested her cane against the settee. "I'm so happy to finally meet you, Lily. I've heard so much about you. And Rosalia, you sweet child. You're practically still a bride. You and Elmo just married this past winter, haven't you?"

"Yes, we have," Rosalia said.

"I've been a victim of lumbago, holed up in my home for some time now, but Camelia here has been nursing me with her herbs."

"Oh, I know what miracles she performs. You don't have to tell me about that," Lily said, as she waved her palm.

"Will you please excuse me while I go to the kitchen and see about dinner?" Camelia looked at both of her friend's eyes for approval.

"Of course, *chere*. Melba and I will get acquainted," Lily said.

Camelia found Dominique in the kitchen, struggling to carry the large roasting pan out of the oven to the stovetop. "Do you think the lamb is done, *mere?*" His black moustache and goatee bobbed up and down, as he sniffed the gingery aroma permeating the air.

"It should be. Will you help me lift it to this platter, Dom?" They lifted the sizzling leg of lamb from the roasting pan with two large spatulas. The crusty roasted leg plopped down on the large platter, splattering hot grease across the black, cast iron stove top.

Dominique wet his lips and slapped his hands together in anticipation. He slid one slice off the lamb leg and scrutinized it. "It looks *parfait*. I'll slice it, *mere*, if you'd like me to."

Camelia gave him a smile of approval and a nod.

"Mamma, the gravy's hot and smooth. I covered it to keep warm," Collette said.

Bubba darted between the women's legs and stood at Dominique's feet, staring up at the meat. His long tail wagged back and forth.

Camelia shook a finger at the big, gray cat. "Bubba, if you don't stop running around this kitchen between our legs, I'm going to put you in the bedroom with the door closed."

"Mamma, someone's at the door. I know you love to receive your guests. Dominique and I can dish the vegetables up and put them on the table. You go ahead."

"You're such a blessing, Collette. What would I do without you and Dominique? Oh, and Dom, Collette told me your wonderful news. I'm so happy I could kiss you both. I'll have to attend to that later. I don't even have time to scratch my arm. The vegetables are hot in the oven."

Camelia scurried to her front door to find Katia and Justice. "Oh, Katia, our newest bride! I'm so happy you could make it with your new husband. You must be Justice." She grabbed his hand and looked into his eyes. "You are a handsome devil if I must say so myself." She cackled, as she embraced the newly married couple.

As they entered Camelia's parlor, Camelia said, "Katia, you know Miss Lily, Rosalia's mother-in-law."

"Why, yes, Miss Lily. And this is my husband, Justice."

Justice stood tall and bowed to the ladies. "It's good to meet you, Miss Lily. And you must be Rosalia."

"However did you know?"

"My wife has described you to a tee."

"Oh, this is my good friend, Melba. I've known her for ages," Camelia said.

Justice bowed to the matron. "How do you do, madame."

Rosalia rushed up to Katia and embraced her. "I'm so glad you could spend Easter with us. I'm bursting to tell you something later," she whispered.

Katia reached down for Blossom Rose. "Is this Blossom, the youngest of La Fonda's?" My, how she's grown since I last saw her."

Blossom put her head on Katia's shoulder. "Want my mamma."

"Yes, the children are beside themselves today. They're so excited about their mamma coming home," Rosalia said. "I'd better see if my sister needs my help getting the food on the table. Mamma's so excited about having her friends over, I don't think she's thinking about the food."

As Collette and Rosalia brought bowls of vegetables and dressing to the table, Rosalia's undisguised joy could not be hidden from Collette. "You look mighty happy today, Sister,"

"Yes, I've every reason to be happy. I'm doubly happy."

"Doubly? And why is that?" Collette rushed back to the kitchen from the dining room.

"Because our children will play together, Sister! Can you beat that?"

Collette turned to look at her sister who looked happier than she ever remembered with a glow on her face. "Oh, you mean that you're going to have a baby?"

"Yes. Our children will be one month apart. Mamma will be busy, won't she?" They both giggled.

"I'm so happy for you, Rosalia, but why haven't you told me sooner?"

"When you called to tell me of your good news, I wanted to be sure I was pregnant. I hadn't even told Elmo yet. Besides, I didn't want to burst your bubble needlessly. You sounded so happy. I just wanted to hear you talk about your sweet little baby that you wanted so much."

Hugging her sister, Collette was near tears. "No, I'm not going to cry. This is a double happy occasion. Let's get the food on the table."

Camelia viewed her daughters from the dining room. She smiled to herself at the sight of her girls embracing. As she walked into the kitchen, she said, "What a lovely sight. Sisterly love. Is there a special reason today?"

"Our children will play together, Mamma." Collette gave her mother a big grin, as she left the kitchen with a basket of hot rolls.

"You're with child, Rosalia?"

"Yes, Mamma." Rosalia beamed with joy.

"That's wonderful news. I'm so excited," Camelia said, as she hugged Rosalia. "I have to put the coffee on now lest I forget later. Rosalia, will you take this other basket of hot rolls to the table, and the butter, too?" She sent a chirping kiss to Rosalia.

As she put a match to the burner and put the coffee pot on the fire, she noticed something white move in the corner of her kitchen near the back door. She was aware that her dead husband, Claudio, was watching her put coffee into her white, enamel percolator. "Claudio. I've been so busy today. How long have you been standing there?"

"Oh, I've been watching you for quite some time, Camelia."

"Did you hear? We're going to be grandparents. I'm so happy."

"That's lovely, Camelia. I have something I want to tell you, *chere.*"

"Yes?"

"Now that you're going to have grandchildren of your very own, it's time to start a new phase of your life without me. I know you'll be a wonderful grandmother and you'll help your daughters raise their children to be as fine as your daughters. I don't want to be in the way of this. You've mourned me for seventeen years. Live the happy life you deserve without me."

"Oh, Claudio, you look so handsome in that white suit you wore at our wedding. You mean I won't get to see you any more?"

"No, Camelia. Start your life as a grandmother in happiness. It's time for you to stop grieving me. You've helped so many people to be happy. Be happy yourself. Just remember how much I loved you. That's all. Goodbye, my love."

She wiped one tear with her apron. "Good-bye, Claudio. Good-bye, my sweet husband. I love you, too. Always will."

She heard the squeals of the children and rushed to the parlor. Through the front window, she saw Andre helping La Fonda from the carriage. "Oh, my land, she's skinnier than ever!"

"I gotta see my mamma!" Gossie ran out the front door with his sisters following.

"Mamma! Mamma!" Blossom yelled in excitement.

"Oh, be careful now, Blossom. Don't run down those stairs lest you fall and hurt yourself." Camelia stood on her front porch, watching the children run to La Fonda.

La Fonda fought back tears, as she bent down to get a better look at them. The children put their arms around her. "Oh, I want to kiss you, Gossie, Geetie, and Blossom. I really do, but mamma's afraid I'd make you sick."

Gossie grinned at his mother. "Oh, Mamma, you wouldn't make us sick. I go to school now, Mamma."

"I know, and I understand you've been a very good boy for *tante*. Oh, I love you for that, Gossie. And I love you, Geetie."

"Too, Mamma?" Blossom looked up to her mother with arms outstretched.

"Yes, you too, Blossom. I love you too, and I missed you so much. Oh, there's *Tante* Camelia. Yoohoo, *Tante*." La Fonda waved in excitement.

La Fonda climbed the stairs with the aid of Andre. "Miss Camelia, I'm so happy to be here. I won't kiss you even though I'd love to."

"Happy Easter, child. This Easter is so special with you here. And Andre, you can kiss me, can't you?" Camelia said.

"My pleasure, *Tante* Camelia. Happy Easter." Andre kissed his aunt on the cheek and embraced her.

"Come in and meet all of my friends. I think you know most of them. I don't know if you've met my friend, Melba."

Melba extended her hand for a handshake. "How do you do, Andre. I've heard so much about you and La Fonda."

Andre walked over and kissed Melba's hand. "Any friend of my *tante's* is a friend of mine. My pleasure to meet you. And this is my wife, La Fonda. You've met Gossie, Geetie, and Blossom Rose, I presume."

"Andre, Katia, our newest bride, is here with her husband, Justice," Camelia said.

"I'm so pleased to see you again, Katia. Justice." He shook hands with Justice and kissed Katia's hand.

"Madame Lily, it's lovely to spend Easter with you." He kissed her hand.

"The pleasure is all mine, Andre."

Dominique entered the dining room with a large, handled meat platter and a smile on his face. "Happy Easter, everyone."

"I believe dinner is served now that my dear son-in-law has carved the lamb. Let us all adjourn to the dining room. La Fonda, you sit first. You shouldn't be standing. Sit here, *chere*. Andre, you can sit next to your wife. Lily, next to my place. Yes, that's a good place for you, Katia and Justice. Now that we're all seated, Andre, would you like to say grace?"

"I would rather you say grace, T*ante*. You always say grace so much more personal than I.

"Very well." Camelia closed her eyes and folded her hands. "Dear Lord, this family has been so blessed by your graces. You've answered our prayers. My dear daughter, Rosalia, is a happy wife with her loving husband, Elmo, and will be a mother. Thank you, Jesus!"

"Thank you, Jesus!" the guests prayed with eyes closed and hands folded in prayer.

"And my daughter, Collette, and her lovely husband, Dominique, are expecting a baby. Thank you, Jesus!"

"Thank you, Jesus!" the guests prayed.

"And my dear friend, Lily, and I will be grandmothers together."

"Oh, thank you, Jesus!" Camelia held back a sob, as her guests thanked in unison.

"Thank you, Jesus!" Lily squeezed Camelia's hand in excitement.

"My friend, Melba here, couldn't walk outside at all. She has regained her strength to walk again with less pain. Thank you, Jesus!"

"Oh, thank you, Jesus!" Melba prayed above the rest.

"And my dear friend, Katia, who I've known since she was a wee child and was a lost soul who thought she would never meet a man who would love her. She has found happiness with a fine man, and now they're married. Thank you, Jesus!"

"Thank you, Jesus!" the guests proclaimed.

"And Gossie, my great-nephew. I'm so proud of you, Gossie. You are a blessing to our family. You go to school and you study hard, and you teach your sister everything that you learn in school. You watch over your sisters. And Geetie, you are the best big sister. You always watch that your baby sister is safe. This family thanks God for you children."

"Thank you, Jesus!" The guests raised their voices.

"And La Fonda, my good little mother here, has been working so hard to take care of her three children. She has never wanted anything but for her children to be healthy and happy and for Gossie to go to school. And she has wanted health for herself so that she could take care of her family. Please keep her healthy, dear sweet Jesus!"

"Please, sweet Jesus!" the guests implored.

"And last but not least, my favorite nephew. Andre and I were praying that he get a teaching position so that he could get better living quarters for his family. And God sent down a job for him from heaven. He's teaching math and philosophy. Thank you, Jesus! Thank you for blessing this family."

"Thank you, Jesus!" Andre's voice quivered, as the dinner guests' voices drowned his out.

"What about you, Mamma?" Rosalia looked at her mother.

"I've got everything I asked for." Camelia smiled back at her daughter.

"Even that last thing we talked about?"

"Yes, God has granted me a joyous heart. I have everything I want. Thank you God for my family and my friends. Alleluia! Alleluia!"

"Alleluia! Alleluia!"